Say Yes

Also by Donna Hill

If I Could

Heat Wave (with Niobia Bryant and Zuri Day)

Say Yes

Donna Hill

DAFINA BOOKS
Kensington Publishing Corp.
http://www.kensingtonbooks.com

DAFINA BOOKS are published by

Kensington Publishing Corp.
119 West 40th Street
New York, NY 10018

All Kensington Titles, Imprints, and Distributed Lines are
available at special quantity discounts for bulk purchases for
sales promotions, premiums, fund-raising, and educational or
institutional use. Special book excerpts or customized print-
ings can also be created to fit specific needs. For details, write
or phone the office of the Kensington special sales manager:
Kensington Publishing Corp., 119 West 40th Street, New York,
NY 10018, attn: Special Sales Department, Phone: 1-800-221-
2647.

Dafina and the Dafina logo Reg. U.S. Pat. & TM Off.

ISBN-13: 978-1-61773-107-5
ISBN-10: 1-61773-107-2

First Dafina mass market printing: August 2004
10 9 8 7 6

Printed in the United States of America

Prologue

All during the ride to Parker's apartment in SoHo, Regina kept replaying Parker's last comment as they left Victoria and Phillip's home on Long Island. What in the world did he mean by "maybe not"? She dared not ask. She dared not court another disappointment. She'd had enough of those things to last her three lifetimes. So she dared not ask. That was a threshold she wasn't ready to cross. But her curiosity was killing her.

Once they were inside and settled, Parker surprised her by opening a bottle of chilled imported champagne. He poured two fingers of the amber liquid into a pair of fluted glasses and handed one to her.

"To you, Regina, for fighting the odds and beating them." He raised his glass in a toast, then stopped. "And to us. I hope this is the beginning of something enduring."

She gently tapped her glass against his.

Parker took her free hand and led her to the gray

leather sectional couch. What he felt for her at that moment was reflected in the sensual heat in his eyes. Gently, he draped his arm around her shoulder, his gaze locked on hers.

"There's something I want to tell you." His voice wavered a bit but quickly regained its power.

Uh-oh. "What is it?"

After seating her, Parker sat down where he could continue to read her face. "I've been doing a lot of thinking lately about us, about me, and what I want to do with my life. What I discovered, Regina, is that I really want you with me. Watching you these past few months made me see just what can be accomplished when you believe in yourself. Something I haven't done in a long time. I've let what happened to me and Lynn color everything I did, how I functioned, the choices that I made. I'd forgotten that happiness was still possible, that I still had something to offer. You made me see that with your encouragement and your caring. But the only way I can be the man that you deserve is to finally put my past to rest."

Her heart tumbled over in her chest. "How?" she whispered.

"I'd given up on trying to find my daughter," he replied. "More out of fear as time went along than anything else."

"What are you afraid of?"

"Afraid that I won't measure up. Afraid that when I did find her she wouldn't care about me one way or the other. Afraid that she'll believe I abandoned her, that I didn't love her enough to fight for her. Afraid that she won't believe how much I love and miss her."

Her expression softened. She tenderly stroked

his cheek, brushed his locks away from the side of his face. "The one thing I've learned through all of this, from my friends, from my family, from my own mistakes, is that fear is our greatest enemy. And the only way to conquer it is to face it, no matter how painful, how ugly."

"I know that now. What I want to tell you is, I've found her. I contacted an agency that specializes in reuniting families and she's agreed to see me. They have contacts and sources nationwide. I don't know how it's all going to turn out, but it's a start."

"Oh, Parker, I'm so happy for you. I know how much your daughter means to you. It'll work out. And even if it doesn't turn out exactly the way you want, you made the effort, you tried, and she'll see that."

"I hope so," he said soberly. "So, I took a short leave of absence from teaching. I'm going to California for a few months. That's where she lives."

"Wow, a few months." She wasn't expecting that. "Well . . ." Her voice trailed off.

"When I come back, and I will, I want us to really work at being a couple. I want to see what it's like to plan a life with someone again. But I know I can't do that, honestly, until that part of my life is settled. What I need to know, Gina, is if that's what you want too."

Did she? Could she totally commit herself to someone again? What if there were more demands made of her than she could fulfill? Could she love someone fully and completely? At times she believed she could. And she thought that Parker could be that person. At other times, she wanted to be selfish, for the first time in her life, and just take care of Regina. But if there was one thing she'd decided when she went on this new adventure in her life it was that she wasn't doing anything the same ever again.

Slowly, she stood, gazed down into Parker's eyes and extended her hand. When he placed his hand in hers, she led him to his bedroom, taking the lead. And that felt good, so good.

In the light and shadow that played through his bedroom window, Regina languidly undressed. She stood before him naked and unguarded, saying with her body what words could not convey.

She was taking a chance with him, she knew that. But what was life without risks? For once, she felt the emotional barriers inside her start to crumble, to give way, and surrendering in this act of passion was not a bad thing. His body yielded its erotic secrets without any play for power or control, seeking only to share and communicate his deep feeling for her. Every caress, every sigh promised her a life so very different than anything she'd ever known. When they kissed so long and so hotly, the electricity they'd both felt the last time surged back through them, validating all of their dreams and fantasies. As she moved above him in a slow, easy rhythm, with no strings, no promises—her head thrown back in ecstasy—her gaze slowly focused on the portrait above his bed.

And there she was captured in all her glory—with an expression that challenged everything before it and said: I can do anything. Yes, I can.

Chapter 1

Regina stretched languidly beneath the cool, pale blue cotton sheet. She turned onto her side and pressed her body against the warm brown flesh of her lover.

She smiled when he murmured her name in his sleep. Their night together was heaven on earth. Parker was a generous lover, catering to her every physical and emotional need, awakening the hidden pleasures of her body. Her years of marriage to Russell Everette may have yielded two beautiful children but it never unleashed the reciprocal passion that Parker elicited from her. It must be the artist in him, she thought with pleasure as a residual tingle ran through her. He used his entire body like a paintbrush, stroking, creating, with her as his canvas.

Regina closed her eyes against the stealth moonlight that peeked through the vertical blinds, signaling the impending dawn of a new day. Inwardly she wished that the night would last forever. At least then she wouldn't have to face leaving Parker, if only temporarily.

Was she falling in love with him? Was she in love with him already? She didn't have the answers yet. She wanted to be sure this time. She'd been reluctant to get involved with anyone again after her divorce. She wanted to work on Regina, making her strong and independent. She wanted to reclaim her personhood, and for the most part she'd done just that. She was single-focused in her goals: building her bookstore business and raising her two teenage children—alone.

But one day fate crossed the threshold of Regina's Place and brought Parker Heywood right along with it, and her life took yet another turn.

Gently, so as not to wake him, she cuddled closer to his warmth and draped her arm across his waist.

A part of her was happy for him and the decision he'd made to reunite with his estranged daughter. She knew how important family was and the hole that was in Parker's heart for losing his. But another part of her, the objective side, had to face the fact that the balance of their still budding relationship was destined to change when his daughter became a part of his life again. For better, for worse, she didn't know. But the one thing she was certain of, bringing a fourteen-year-old young woman into his life after years of separation, was going to take every iota of time and patience that Parker could summon.

Regina sighed, released her hold of him, and eased out of bed. She wanted to take a quick shower, get dressed, and get home before Michele and Darren got up for school. She was still protective of them when it came to her personal life, and they didn't need to see a man slipping out of her bedroom in the morning, so she'd opted for spending nights at Parker's place, which was an issue in and of itself.

"Where are you going?" Parker mumbled, his deep voice still thick and sexy with sleep.

"Gotta get home," she said in a whisper.

Parker pulled himself up to a semisitting position and rubbed his eyes. "How long do you plan to keep our relationship a secret from your children?"

"I'm not keeping us a secret. There's nothing wrong with discretion and I don't think it's appropriate for my children to know that I'm sleeping with a man that I'm not married to."

"Do you really think that they believe you're 'out with the girls' when you come tiptoeing in at sunrise in the middle of the week? Kids are pretty wise these days, Gina."

Regina gathered up her discarded clothes and held them against her stomach. She looked him in the eye.

"What they think and what they see are two different things. I'll be curious to see how 'open' you are with your own daughter."

She turned and walked off into the bathroom, shutting the door with a bit more force than necessary.

Regina turned on the shower full blast and quickly stepped under the beating needles of the spray.

That was one of the reasons she didn't want to get involved again, she thought, stamping back the annoyance from Parker's comment. Although she and Russell had been divorced for some years now, she still didn't want the kids to think that someone was trying to take their father's place—at least not yet. They'd been through a great deal over the years and they were still very close to Russell. She was not going to make any more mistakes when it came to her kids and men, and she certainly didn't need them privy to her private sex life.

Regina scrubbed her body with Irish Spring soap, although she would have preferred Dove; she'd have to remind Parker to get some. With her sensitive skin the least little thing set off a wave of dryness and pimples. Unfortunately, at the moment she didn't have much choice. She couldn't very well go home smelling like sex.

Was she being too old-fashioned? she worried as she lathered and rinsed. It was important to her that Michele and Darren viewed her in a certain light. She had a responsibility to set an example for them.

She turned off the shower and stepped out into the steam-filled room. The mirror was fogged over. She wiped a clean circle with her towel and stared at her reflection. What did her children really think about her weekly rendezvous? And what would she do if Parker grew weary of being her best-kept secret? She exhaled a slow breath of concern, then drew it back in. She'd cross that bridge when she came to it.

Regina reentered the bedroom and picked up

her purse and jacket. She walked to the bed, leaned down, and kissed Parker gently on the lips.

"Talk to you later."

Parker got out of bed, walked naked to the dresser, and pulled out a pair of shorts. He slipped them on as he spoke.

"You know I don't mean to tell you how to run your life and your family."

She nodded. "And I understand how you feel."

He walked up to her and cupped her chin. "We're in this together, babe. And as much as I may or may not like it, I'll stand by your decision. But you gotta know it can't go on like this forever."

Regina inhaled slightly. "I'll work it out. Look, I better go."

"Yeah. . . ."

She walked out and Parker followed her to the front door. "I'll call you this afternoon. Are we still on for later?"

"I'll see how my day is going. Okay?"

"Sure."

She lowered her gaze for a moment. "Bye," she said softly and left.

Parker watched from the window as Regina got into her car and pulled off before he turned away. They'd been seeing each other for months, he mused as he walked into the kitchen and put on the pot for coffee. Regina had not only transformed herself in that time, but transformed him as well. Since his divorce from Lynn and imposed separation from his daughter, Tracy, he'd buried himself in his art and in teaching, leaving little room or time for a relationship. Then he met Regina and all the promises he'd made to himself to stay clear of women went out the window. Before he knew what was happening, he was opening himself up again, allowing himself to feel. But it was getting harder to keep himself in the background of her life and he wondered if the reasons were really the kids or something else.

Regina quietly slipped her key into the lock of her front door, feeling like a cat burglar in her own home. She held her breath as she heard the locks click and the door squeak open. The last person she expected to see was sitting in her kitchen. She swallowed hard and closed the door behind her.

"What are you doing here, Russell?"

Russell put down his coffee mug and checked his watch. He gazed at her with veiled jealousy in his cool brown eyes.

"A better question is, why weren't you here?"

Regina walked fully into the room and dropped her purse on the kitchen table with a clatter.

Her hazel eyes narrowed. "The last time I checked, my name was the only one on the lease."

"And the last time I checked, our children were still underage." Russell stood, his broad, imposing physique towering over her. "If you want to spend the night out doing . . . whatever . . . that's your business. But when your running around affects Michele and Darren, then it becomes my business."

Regina defiantly folded her arms and rested her weight on her right leg. "I think you need to leave. Now."

Russell reached for the coffee cup and drained it. "I'm not going to allow you to screw up their heads, Regina."

"Allow! We're not married anymore, Russell. Your days of 'allowing' me to do anything are long over. And you're right, my private life is my private business. And if you know nothing else about me, you know I would never do anything to hurt the kids."

Russell crossed the room and put his cup in the sink. He turned toward her.

"I think you need to get your priorities in order. If the kids are as important to you as you claim they are, then you need to start acting like it."

He snatched up his jacket from the back of the chair and draped it over his arm. Russell lowered his head a minute in thought, then looked at Regina.

"Look, I don't want to be a hard-ass. I don't want to interfere in your life. You're right, we aren't married anymore, and I regret that every day that I open my eyes." He shifted his weight and his voice softened. "I still care about you, Regina. And to be honest . . . it bugs me to even imagine you with another man."

Regina tried to hide her shock and embarrassment behind a bland expression. The last person she wanted to have a conversation with about her love life was her ex-husband or to hear him confess any feelings for her.

"Anyway," Russell continued, "whatever you may think about me, think about the kids too." Russell walked to the door. "Have a good day."

Regina stood in the center of her red and white checkerboard kitchen, held in place by disbelief. To walk into her home after a night of toe-curling lovemaking to find your ex-husband sitting in your kitchen was mind-numbing. And she had yet to deal with her kids.

It wouldn't be the first time Michele and Darren felt they could run her life better than she could. Shortly after her divorce from Russell and after she'd decided to quit her job and open the bookstore, they'd gotten her mother all twisted up in her life. Her mother, who always adored Russell, went on a personal campaign to get them back together and she had the help of her grandchildren.

Regina shook her head, scattering the thoughts and images of those trying days. She'd come too far to assert herself and her total independence to be corralled back into a life of complacency—pleasing everyone except herself.

She looked around her cozy home, the space that she'd created for her and the kids—her sanctuary. When she'd left Russell, all she took was clothes and her bank account. Everything from the short, white kitchen curtains, the sconces that hung on the living room walls, the quilts and throw rugs, to the brass coatrack in the hallway—it was all hers. And she didn't need anyone's permission.

Regina proceeded down the hallway to her bedroom, tossing aside her flirt with apprehension and guilt.

She went in, sat on the side of the bed, and took off her shoes. When she looked up, her gaze rested on the photograph of her and the kids, and Russell's barely concealed words of condemnation sprang back into her head. She ran her fingers through her jaw-length auburn locks and pushed the thoughts aside. She certainly didn't need any foolishness out of Russell. She had no idea what his agenda really was, but she had enough drama in her life already without Russell adding to the mix.

Both of her best friends, Toni and Victoria, were up to their eyeballs in drama and she was doing the best she could to be there for them. And the best way to do that was to keep her personal drama at a bare minimum.

Regina stood and stretched, enjoying the way her body sweetly ached after being loved up by Parker.

He was right, she grudgingly admitted. She had been shielding the kids from him. But she wanted to be careful. She wanted to be sure of where she and Parker were going before integrating him into the lives of Michele and Darren. She'd overheard stories from customers in her bookstore who'd traipsed one man after another through the lives of their children and then couldn't understand why they started acting out negatively.

Children needed stability, she reasoned, reaching for the remote to tune into *The Today Show*—her favorite morning program. And one man after another like taxis in Midtown Manhattan was not the example she wanted to set.

Although sometimes she did feel like a sneaky teenager going to meet the boyfriend the parents refused to let her see. But the bottom line was, Parker Heywood had fed her starving sexuality and she had no intention of going back to her starvation diet.

Until she reached the point where they were making plans for a forever, she was going to keep their relationship on the DL.

Regina stretched out on the bed just as she heard the faint sound of Michele's followed by Darren's alarm clock. She leaned back against her plumped-up pillows and crossed her arms beneath her breasts. She had a serious bone to pick with both of them. She was going to find out who called Russell and why.

Chapter 2

Antoinette Devon prepared for work. She had a full caseload at the clinic and she needed to get in early to be prepared. As a social worker she was adept at solving the problems of others, finding resources and safe havens. Her life was a different story, however.

She quickly brushed a few strokes of mascara to her lashes and noticed that her hair needed a touch-up. She made a mental note to make an appointment for Friday after work.

There was a time when Friday nights were reserved for "the girls." She, Regina, and Victoria would meet up after work and commiserate about their lives and loves. Those were the days, she thought a bit wistfully, that were no more. Regina was busy with her new love and her new business. Victoria was busy being pregnant and her . . . well, she was simply trying to get from one day to the next.

Antoinette turned from the mirror and crossed

the pristine bedroom to the closet. She stood in the open doorway scanning the rows of designer suits and dresses. On the rack on the floor was a row of shoes from every famous maker. She decided on a simple Donna Karen navy suit and matching pumps.

If only her life could be as well designed as her attire and her home, she mused, slipping on the jacket over a sleeveless pale pink top of raw silk. She had no one to blame but herself. She put on her shoes and took her purse from the top shelf of the well-organized closet. Her illicit affair with Alan, a former client, had ruined her marriage and now jeopardized her parental rights for her son, Steven.

Antoinette straightened her shoulders and drew in the tears that were never far from falling. Months had passed and Charles was no closer to forgiving her now than he was when he found out. Her stomach muscles knotted. She couldn't blame him.

To the world it appeared that Antoinette Devon had it all: a solid career, a beautiful three-story brownstone, a great wardrobe, and a new car every year. But things were so far from perfect. All day she listened to the problems of others. She only wished that there was someone she could pour her heart out to.

She picked up her car keys from the dresser and headed out. If she didn't run into traffic she would be sitting at her desk in forty-five minutes.

Antoinette slowly stood up behind her desk and stretched following the departure of her first client of the morning. It was a grueling hour but she felt confident that she'd made progress. She glanced

down at the open case folder on her desk: Leslie
Cummings, age seventeen, expelled from school
for attacking another student. Leslie claimed self-
defense but school records showed that she had a
long history of violence—in the home and out.
She'd been coming to see Antoinette for six weeks,
but today was the first time Antoinette felt as if
she'd gotten through to her. At the core of Leslie's
anger were issues of abandonment, first her father,
then her mother, then the father of her two-year-
old son.

Antoinette flipped the folder closed and sighed
deeply. What Leslie was dealing with was what
Antoinette feared for her own son. Steven had become withdrawn and belligerent since Charles
moved out, making an almost unmanageable situation that much more difficult. But, truth be told,
Steven's problems began before Charles left. She
still shuddered when she thought about the night
they had to pick him up from the police precinct—
the very same day Charles had discovered her infi-
delity. She only hoped that somehow with all her
training and experience she could apply it to her
own life and save her son before she lost him for
good.

The light tap on her office door drew her away
from her dark musings.

"Yes, come in," she called out, as she put on "the
good face."

"Mrs. Devon, there's an Alan Pierre here to see
you," her secretary said, while poking her head in
the door. "He doesn't have an appointment but he
said he was a former client and that it was important that he speak with you."

Antoinette's temples immediately began to pound

in concert with her suddenly racing heart. Alan. She hadn't seen him since that fateful day and had only spoken to him on the phone to explain that she couldn't see him anymore. Why was he here now?

She cleared her throat and debated the veracity of seeing him at all. But it might be important, her professional voice whispered, when all the while her heart hoped otherwise. She checked her watch. She had fifteen minutes before her next client was due.

"Tell him to come in, but make it clear that I only have a few minutes."

Antoinette tugged on the bottom of her jacket and ran her fingers through her hair. Was her lipstick still in place? she worried, or worse, on her teeth? She ran her tongue across them just to be sure as the knock came on her door.

She took a deep breath and planted an innocuous expression on her face. "Come in." She looked up as Alan walked through the door, and in that instant all the anguish that she'd endured as a result of their affair went out the window.

Alan closed the door behind him and stood in place. "Hello, Toni."

Her heart was beating so quickly she could barely catch her breath. "Alan. This is a surprise." Slowly she stood and wished that she hadn't when she realized how badly her legs were trembling.

"I know we said we wouldn't see each other or call, but . . ." His gaze shifted around the room, then settled on her. "I miss you, Toni. Very much. And I needed to see for myself that you were okay."

She laughed without humor. "I haven't been okay in a very long time," she said, resignation weighing down her voice. "Have a seat," she said, extending her hand toward the empty chair opposite her desk.

Alan crossed the room and sat.

For several moments they stared at each other in an awkward silence.

"Did you and . . . Charles work things out?" he finally asked.

She shook her head. "He . . . uh . . . moved out." She clasped her hands together on top of the desk.

"Toni . . . I'm so sorry. Sorry about everything."

"So am I." She gave him a sad smile. "How have you been?"

"Getting there, one day at a time. It's harder without you."

"Alan, don't—"

"Wait." He held up his hand. "Just hear me out. When you told me that Charles found out, I was hurting for you. I wanted to be there for you. But I understood that you needed to try to work things out." He unbuttoned his jacket and leaned forward, bracing his arms on his thighs. He looked directly into her eyes. "But there was also a part of me that was happy that it happened. I was tired of living a lie, sneaking around with . . . the woman I'd fallen in love with."

"Alan—"

"I wasn't asking for that in return from you. I knew you had a husband . . . a family. But I want you to know that if you ever decide that you want to try to make things work between us—I'm willing." He stood up abruptly. "That's all I came to say." He gave her a crooked smile. "The number is still the same if you decide you want to use it." He turned and walked out, closing the door gently behind him.

Antoinette stared at the closed door for what felt like an eternity. Her thoughts were racing in every conceivable direction at once. *Work things out . . . in love with me . . .*

She couldn't get involved with Alan. What if Charles changed his mind and decided he wanted to come back? He'd never trust her again.

She pressed her clenched fist to her mouth and glanced at the door again. Who was she kidding? Charles wasn't coming back. If anything, he wanted to stay as far away from her as possible and take Steven with him.

The number is still the same if you decide you want to use it.

"Your next client is here, Ms. Devon," her assistant said, mysteriously appearing in front of her.

Antoinette blinked.

"Are you okay?"

"Uh . . . yes." She forced a smile and uttered a laugh that sputtered with weak energy. She pushed some papers aside on her desk and picked up the next case file in the stack. "Walter can come in now." She tried to clear her head, but Alan's visit and parting words held her in an invisible grip. *Why now, Alan, when I'm so lonely, so needy? Why now?*

Chapter 3

Clad only in a pair of blue and white boxers, Parker rummaged around in his black and white art deco kitchen in search of something to eat. As usual after a long night of lovemaking, especially with Regina, he awoke ravenous.

He took out some eggs and a platter of leftover fresh ham and placed them on the counter. He reached up over the stainless steel sink and switched on the radio. The announcer was briefing the listening audience on the latest celebrity drama that ended up in the court of law. He shook his head in disgust as much as dismissal. Although he longed for the day when his art would be recognized enough so that it totally sustained him, he never wanted to reach the heights of celebrity where every iota of your life was constantly under a microscope, viewed and reviewed for all the world to see and judge.

Parker beat two eggs in a cerulean porcelain bowl, took his favorite carving knife, and cut thin slices of ham. He leaned his hip against the counter as he sipped his coffee and absently watched the ham sizzle in the pan.

Eating breakfast alone again. He would have much preferred to be standing in his kitchen with Regina at his side, inhaling that soft scent that floated around her when she was fresh from sleep. He loved the way her skin felt like silk in the morning and the dreamy look that her hypnotic hazel eyes held. He wanted to sit opposite her at the table as they ate and talked about their plans for the day—the plans for their life. Instead, she was tiptoeing out of his bed under the cloak of a breaking dawn—and he was alone.

"Damn it!" He snapped out of his musing, grabbed a fork, and plucked the much-too-crisp piece of ham from the pan and tossed the blackened debris in the garbage. "Great start to the day," he grumbled as he scrubbed the pan with water and steel wool before setting it back on the stove.

Just as he was about to turn on the flame and put another piece of ham in the skillet and try again, the phone rang. He turned and crossed the black opal Italian marble floor to the cordless phone mounted on the wall near the window. It was barely nine A.M.

"Hello?"

"Parker, it's Lynn."

He frowned. It took a moment for his brain to make any kind of connection between the voice and the name. "Lynn? Is something wrong?" It was barely six in the morning on the West Coast. His ex-wife hadn't called him in more years than he could count, and at this hour it could only be trouble.

"I figured you'd be up," she said in the same

husky voice that he'd memorized and then tried to forget. "Old habits die hard."

"I'm pretty sure you didn't call me to discuss my old habits or the time of day." The sting of what she'd done still lingered in his head, in his heart, and in his voice. "Is something wrong with Tracy?"

He heard the sound of papers rustling and the distinct sound of a glass breaking in the background.

Lynn spat out a string of curses. "Sorry," she mumbled. "Been really clumsy lately." She released a nervous-sounding laugh.

A wave rose in his stomach, then settled. He crossed the room and sat down at the table. "What is it, Lynn?" He kept his voice level, hoping he carefully hid his growing sense of dread.

She made a big deal of clearing her throat. "I know you plan to come down and see Tracy."

"Yes . . . is that going to be a problem? We discussed this—"

"I know, I know," she snapped. "That was always your problem, Parker."

"And what problem might that be, Lynn? According to you I had so many I've lost count," he tossed back.

"Forget it," she said, an uncharacteristic note of resignation in her tone.

Parker's antenna went back up. In all the years that he'd known and lived with Lynn, she'd never backed down from an argument, no matter how minute.

"Why don't we stop trying to beat each other up and talk about why you called?"

A good ten seconds of silence hummed over the phone lines. Finally, Lynn spoke.

"Tracy is going to need to stay with you for a while. Maybe longer than a while."

She wasn't making sense. "You mean longer than spring break? What are you talking about?"

"I don't know if . . . if Tracy will be able to come back home."

Parker stood. "Lynn, what the hell is going on?"

"I'm really sorry for everything, Parker. For leaving the way I did, for not letting Tracy have her father in her life, for being bitter and angry all these years." Her voice hitched. "She needs you."

Parker paced as he listened, trying to make sense of what she was saying. He didn't want to give voice to the dark thoughts that were forming in his head. But he needed to know. He deserved to know.

"I want you to tell me right now, what is going on?" He heard her stifle a sob. "Lynn, for God's sake, talk to me! For once talk to me." He wanted to jump through the phone and shake her into speaking.

"I have about six months to a year, the doctors say."

Parker felt as if his heart momentarily ceased to beat. "Lynn . . ."

"I . . . don't want Tracy around for that. This is a good time for her to get to know her father, don't you think?" She tried to laugh but it came out more like a strangled cry.

"Lynn . . . what doctors have you seen? Are they sure?"

"I've seen more doctors than I can count. What do they say? They all say the same damned thing." She drew in a long breath. "When you come down in two weeks, I'll have spoken to her about her staying in New York to finish her junior year of high school."

"Does she know?"

"No."

"You need to tell her."

"No."

"This is not something to keep from her. She needs to know."

"No."

"Don't be ridiculous. What is she supposed to think . . . when . . . ?"

"I won't tell her. I can't. If I do she'll want to stay here, and I won't allow that. I'll tell her when she gets settled up there with you. At least she will have you to turn to."

"Lynn—"

"Don't, okay? I don't want or need your sympathy. I need you to take care of our daughter. Let me know your flight time and we'll be there to pick you up at the airport."

"If that's the way you want it." He paused. "I'll call you."

"Good-bye, Parker."

Before he could respond she hung up. He held the phone in his hand for several moments before returning it to the base. In a daze he walked out of the kitchen.

Chapter 4

Regina slid off the bed and headed back out into the kitchen. Knowing her children the way she did, she was aware that it was only a matter of time before they would find their way into the refrigerator and cabinets in search of something quick to eat on the run.

She made herself comfortable at the kitchen table and waited.

Like clockwork, Darren appeared first and his sister was right behind him. Regina's expression was stoic as she tried to keep in mind that she loved these people she'd birthed even if right at that moment she wanted to strangle them.

"Have a seat. Both of you," she instructed without preamble.

The siblings, almost exact replicas of their father, stole a glance at each other before pulling up seats.

"Whose idea was it to call your father?" She looked from one to the other. "I want an answer."

"I told her not to call," Darren blurted.

Michele punched him in the arm. "Traitor."

"I already knew. I was just waiting for confirmation." Regina folded her arms on the tabletop. "You want to tell me why, Michele?"

Michele cut her eyes, pursed her mouth, and slouched in the chair.

"Sit up and answer me when I'm talking to you!"

Michele breathed rapidly and with great reluctance did as her mother instructed. She stared down at the hand-painted place mat in front of her.

Regina glanced at her son. "Go finish getting dressed."

"I'm already dressed," he protested. "I'm hungry."

"Well, your belly is going to have to wait a minute. Go into your room until I call you. I want to talk to your sister."

"Ma! I'm gonna starve to death."

"I doubt it, Darren. Now go."

"Aw, man . . ." He grumbled as he got up and stalked back to his room.

Regina focused her attention on her daughter, who seemed to be determined to look at anything but her.

"Why, Michele?"

Michele tossed her mother a look of pure contempt. "You were gone and I didn't know where you were."

"Michele, I told you I was going out. If you were that concerned you have my cell number; you could have called me."

"I didn't want to *disturb* you," she said, the sarcasm as sharp as a sudden slap in the face.

"What is that supposed to mean?"

Michele turned all her attention and her seventeen-year-old anger on her mother. "You tell me. You were the one who was out all night! You left us here to be with him!" Her eyes suddenly welled with tears. She tugged in several short, quick breaths and held the tears in check.

"Michele." Regina's voice softened. "What is it that you are so upset about? Really?"

"I don't like Parker. I don't think he's right for you."

Regina was stunned. "What? Why would you say something like that?"

"I just don't like him. I'm entitled to my opinion, aren't I?"

"What has Parker ever done but be decent to you and your brother? You barely know him."

"And I don't want to know him," she said, sulking.

"Michele, listen to me." She reached across the table and took Michele's balled fist and covered it with her hand. "I care about Parker. I want to spend time with him. Just like you want to spend time with your friends."

"But does it have to be him?"

"I really don't understand your resentment, Michele. It's not making sense."

"You would take his side."

"Side? I'm not taking sides, I'm trying to understand." She was becoming more baffled and frustrated by the minute.

"You don't understand anything I say anyway."

"Since when? We're both speaking the same language, aren't we?"

Michele shrugged her shoulders. Regina tried another approach.

"What were you hoping to accomplish by calling your father?"

"At least he was here. We can depend on him to be around."

Regina chuckled derisively. "How soon we forget," she said sadly, remembering the days that turned into months, then years that Russell was out of their life of his own choosing and how that affected Michele and Darren. She'd run out of excuses as to why their father didn't come to see them, so she stopped trying to explain. And now that he was back, it was as if all that time, the pain never happened and she was suddenly the villain.

"You know what, Michele? I really thought we'd gotten past this, but it's apparent that we haven't. But this is how things are: I'm a grown woman, this is my house, and I can come and go as I choose. I don't answer to you or your brother. You two answer to me. And the very next time you feel the need to call your father to report on me—don't. I'm not going to stand for it. I give you respect as a young woman, I expect no less in return." She paused. "I hope we understand each other."

Michele didn't respond.

"Do we understand each other?"

"Yes," she hissed out from between her teeth.

"Good. Go and finish getting ready for school and tell your brother he can come and get something to eat now."

Michele pushed up from the chair with such force it wobbled, then settled back in place. She gave her mother one last look and stormed off.

Regina lowered her head to her folded arms and closed her eyes. She had no idea if she'd come close to reaching her daughter. For the life of her she couldn't understand Michele's sudden animosity toward Parker.

Sure there was some friction in the beginning, when Russell reappeared in their lives and the kids wanted him to get back together with their mother. But she was sure they were beyond that. They'd said they wanted her to be happy and if that meant not getting back with Russell they understood. Why the three-sixty?

Slowly she raised her head and looked in the direction of the hallway where the bedrooms were lined up. If Michele and Darren were truly, wholeheartedly against her being with Parker, what chance did they stand as a couple? Could she in good conscience continue in a relationship with a man that her children were so strongly opposed to?

She slapped her palm against the table, then pressed the heel of it to her forehead. "When is my life going to get just a little bit easy?"

Regina was behind the counter in her bookstore when the bell over the front door rang. She glanced up from the inventory list she was checking as Antoinette walked in, looking totally put together as always. Regina closed the folder and came from behind the counter with a smile and an embrace of welcome. It had been weeks since she'd seen Antoinette.

"Hey, girl. Who's taking care of the patients if you're out roaming the streets?" Regina held Antoinette for a moment before releasing her and giving her a total look over. "Sharp as usual," she teased her fashionable friend. "What brings you to my side of the world?"

"I was hoping you had a few minutes."

"Of course." She took Antoinette's hand. "Renee," she called out to her college-student assistant. "Cover the front for me. I'll be in the office." She led Antoinette to the back and let her into the room. "It's a bit cluttered," she said of the stacks of unopened boxes, files, and piles of books to be shelved. "But make yourself comfortable. Can I get you anything?"

"No, thanks." She found a spot on an over-stuffed side chair and sat down.

"So . . . what's been going on?"

Antoinette set her purse in her lap, then glanced at Regina. "Of the three of us, you were the one who found a way out of no way."

"No, not really," she said in that self-deprecating way of hers.

"You did. You made choices about your life and went after them and didn't give a damn what anyone thought."

Regina didn't respond, wondering where the conversation was heading. She sat on the edge of the windowsill waiting for her friend to tell her why she'd really come.

"I need your advice."

"Sure. I don't know how much good it will do." She laughed lightly, hoping to ease the slowly building tension in the room. Antoinette didn't laugh in return. If anything she looked as if she was going to burst into tears. "Toni, what's wrong? Is it Charles . . . Steven?"

Antoinette shook her head. "It's Alan."

"Alan?" Regina frowned. "What about him?"

"He came to my office today. He said he still loved me and wanted me back."

"Oh, Toni," Regina dragged out. "What did you tell him?"

"I didn't tell him anything."

"Why the heck not? I thought you were going to try to work things out with Charles."

"Charles." She emitted a pained laugh. "I haven't heard from Charles since he packed up and moved out. My son barely speaks to me." A single tear slid down her cheek, which she quickly wiped away. "And . . ." She looked across the space into Regina's questioning gaze. "I'm lonely."

"Lonely or horny?"

Antoinette bit back a guilty smile. "Both."

"To-ni!"

She had the decency to look mildly embarrassed. "I know, sad but true."

Regina looked at her friend. Behind the picture-perfect facade, Antoinette was a very unhappy woman. She wished she could find the right words to help Antoinette straighten out her life, but the truth of the matter was that even Antoinette wasn't sure what she wanted out of her life. And until she did, she'd keep making the same mistakes.

"What do you plan to do about Alan?"

Antoinette tugged in a breath. "I don't know. I've worked really hard to put him out of my mind and out of my heart. I wanted things to work between me and Charles. I cut back on my hours at work, I'm home more often." She looked away. "None of that means anything to Charles. He doesn't even come inside the house to see Steven. He has

Steven come outside and then he drives him to the apartment he's been staying in."

"Oh, Toni, I'm so sorry."

"If he wants to hurt me, he's doing a damned good job."

"I don't think that's at the heart of it, T."

Antoinette looked into Regina's eyes. "What do you mean?"

"I may be wrong, but in all the years I've known Charles, I don't know him to be intentionally cruel to anyone." She paused. "But you have to keep in your head that you devastated him by what you did." She saw Antoinette flinch as if the words had a physical presence. "I'm not casting judgment, Toni, but we have to be honest."

"I know," she said in a distant voice. "So what should I do?"

Regina lowered her head, then looked at her friend. "I can't tell you that. You have to do what's in your heart, and hope that it's the right thing for everyone concerned. Give yourself some time, and really think this through."

Antoinette pulled herself up from her seat and clutched her purse in her hand. "I will. Thanks for listening."

Regina hopped down from the sill. "I wish I had the answers for you, sis."

"Yeah, me too." She laughed lightly. "How are things with you and Parker?"

The morning conversation with Michele leaped into her head. "Okay, I guess the usual minor glitches. But they'll work out."

"You're always so positive about things," she said, heading to the door. "I envy that."

"Hmph . . . all smoke and mirrors."

Antoinette laughed and gave Regina a hug. "Talk to you soon."

"Anytime." Regina opened the office door and watched her friend walk out. If only she knew that her life was not nearly as together as it appeared.

She looked around the office to check and see if there was anything that needed her immediate attention when her private line rang. It could only be the kids, her mother, or Parker, she surmised.

"Hello?"

"Hey, babe."

Regina instantly felt warm inside. "Hi," she whispered.

"Listen, about this morning. I was being a real idiot. I have no business telling you how to run your family. I'm sorry."

"No need to apologize. You do have a point and I'm going to work it out. Promise."

"I want to talk to you about something else."

"What?"

"I got a call this morning from Lynn."

Regina's heart beat just a little faster. "Oh." She kept her voice light. "Everything okay?"

"Not really. That's what I want to talk to you about. Face-to-face. I have a full class load today, but I was hoping we could still meet after you close up and have dinner."

"Tonight?"

"Yes."

She was thoughtful for a moment. Two late nights in a row . . . But she was entitled to have a life, too. "Okay . . . uh . . . I close up at the usual time, seven."

"I'll meet you at the store."

"Okay, see you then. Bye."

Regina hung up the phone. The day was already off to a flying start. She didn't want to hazard a guess as to how it would end.

Chapter 5

Victoria sat on the opposite side of the overly or-
nate desk of her immediate supervisor—the senior
vice president—being brought up to date on the
bank's activities since her enforced medical leave
of absence. In the two months that she'd been at
home, nothing much had changed, Victoria realized as Mr. Markowitz droned on, but she kept an
open and interested expression on her face, even
as her mind wandered to other issues.

Phillip had been adamant about her not returning to work at all, she thought. He made enough
money to take care of them, he'd insisted. But Victoria had been just as insistent. If the doctor gave
her clearance to return to work, that's exactly what
she planned to do. She had no intention of spending the next four months sitting on her behind,
getting fat and ugly. In her mind there was nothing
more disagreeable to look at than a big fat black
woman. Every morning she checked her nose to
see if it had spread, and released a breath of relief

to find that it had not. A small thing to any other pregnant mother, but to Victoria it was yet another sign of her *negroness*.

No one truly understood what it was like to be trapped beneath her inky black skin, the unworthiness that she battled daily. For a moment, when she'd fallen down the stairs and nearly lost the baby, she had a major attack of conscience and goodwill. Sure she would go to counseling, she'd promised Phillip. Of course she loved him for who he was, not because he was white, she swore in her hospital bed. Yes, she could love the baby that she carried even if it did come out looking like her—a nightmare she battled valiantly.

But now, back out in the real world without the protection of her perfect home, she was again thrust into the arena of reality, the arena that she fought to be a part of but felt as if she never fit in. And now with the added bulk of her growing belly, she felt even more like an eyesore.

"I think that's about it, Mrs. Hunter," Mr. Markowitz said.

Victoria blinked and brought him back into a clear line of sight. She smiled reflexively. "Thank you," she muttered by rote.

"It's definitely good to have you back," he said, and Victoria knew he was lying. He'd never been good at hiding the fact that he didn't care for having a black woman who was responsible for making major banking decisions. Equal opportunity said he had to keep his ugly thoughts to himself, but Victoria could see the disapproval in his eyes, no matter what came out of his mouth.

Mr. Markowitz stood but he didn't extend his

hand—he never did. "If there's anything you need, be sure to let me know."

"I will. But I'm sure I will be fine."

He nodded.

Victoria stood with as much grace as she could summon and walked out.

On her way back to her office on the second floor, she was stopped every few feet by coworkers welcoming her back and asking how she and "baby" were feeling. By the time she sat down at her desk she was ready to scream. But she didn't have time. There was a stack of mortgages on her desk waiting to be reviewed and approved or denied.

Victoria expelled an exhausted breath and flipped open the first folder in the stack. Before she got past the first page of the financials, her intercom rang.

"Yes?"

"Mrs. Hunter, your husband is on line one," her secretary informed her.

Victoria rolled her eyes. "Thanks, Bridgette." She depressed the flashing red light.

"Hi, Phillip," she said, forcing cheer into her voice.

"Just calling to check on you, sweetheart. How's it going so far?"

"I just got out of an hour-long meeting with the senior vice president and was getting ready to start going through these files."

"Okay, I won't keep you. Just wanted you to know that I was thinking about you."

For a moment her heart softened and she realized that Phillip was only being Phillip—sweet and caring.

"Thanks, I needed that."

"You sound tired, Vicki. Maybe you went back too soon."

"Phillip, we talked this to death." Her moment of compassion disappeared.

"I know that. But it doesn't change the fact that you sound tired and it's not even lunchtime."

She leaned back in her seat and absently massaged her swollen stomach. "I'll be fine. I just need to get back into the swing of things again."

He was momentarily silent. "Don't overdo it. And remember that I'm picking you up after work. We have an appointment with the counselor."

Victoria bit down on her bottom lip. "I really don't see why we have to keep going. What good is it doing?" she snapped.

"It would do us plenty of good if you opened yourself up to it. We made an agreement that we would do this to save our marriage and for your sake as well."

"I know what we agreed to, but things are fine between us and I've come to terms about . . . the baby. So I don't see the point in us continuing to waste our time, not to mention money."

"I really don't think this is the time to get into this. I'll be there to pick you up after work. If that's the way you really feel, then bring it up with Dr. Warner and see what she says."

"Fine, I will."

"Have a nice day, Victoria."

She didn't respond but simply waited for Phillip to hang up and she followed suit.

Victoria briefly shut her eyes, pressed her fingers to her temples, and gently rubbed, trying to dispel the beginnings of a headache—something that was happening more and more frequently.

She hadn't told her obstetrician and she certainly hadn't told Phillip. What she needed to do was relax and stop worrying about the damned baby, that's all. It was no more than that. She glanced down at the gentle rise of her stomach. At least she hoped that's all it was.

Chapter 6

Russell Everette strode out of the conference room and walked alongside his right-hand man, Lenny Townsend, both en route to their next meeting in Washington, D.C.

"I'm going to grab my briefcase and overcoat," Russell said as they approached his corner office. "I'll meet you at the elevator."

Being the timekeeper of the two, Lenny checked his watch. "We have about ten minutes to spare if we want to catch the shuttle out of Kennedy Airport."

"We'll make it. If not, we'll catch the next one. They can't very well have a meeting without us."

"These aren't the kind of folks we want to piss off, Russ."

"Yeah, yeah." He patted Lenny's shoulder. "You worry too much, my man." He jutted his chin in the direction of the exit. "I'll meet you at the elevator."

Lenny nodded and hurried down the hallway.

Russell stopped at his secretary's desk before going into his office.

"Any messages, Lisa?"

"I put them on your desk, Mr. Everette."

"Thanks."

"Do you want me to forward your calls to your cell phone?"

"If it's something you can't handle, fine. If not, I'll just get back to them. I don't foresee anything major cropping up. All the deals that were in negotiations are set. I'll be back tomorrow. Everything straight with my hotel reservations?"

"Yes. You'll be at the Akwaaba Inn."

He smiled. "Love that place," he murmured. He tapped the desk with his palm and hurried into his office. He'd probably killed three of the ten minutes Lenny had allotted him and he really didn't feel like having Lenny tapping his foot and checking his watch all the way to the airport. Lenny was his main man and all, in the office and out, but sometimes he could be a real pain in the ass.

Russell flipped through the messages, noted that there was nothing urgent and shoved them into his jacket pocket, put on his Burberry trench coat, grabbed his briefcase, overnight traveling bag, and laptop. He did a quick once-over of the office and headed out.

"Okay, Lisa, I'm out of here. I'll check in when we land."

"Have a safe trip Mr.—" The phone interrupted her. She held up her index finger, signaling him to wait. "He's right here." She handed him the phone. "It's your daughter."

Russell frowned, glanced down the hall to the elevator, and didn't see Lenny yet. He took the phone.

"What's the matter, baby?"

"Daddy, I want to come and live with you."

He turned his back to his secretary and lowered his voice. "What are you talking about, Michele? Has something happened?"

"I don't want to live here anymore," she whined. "I want you to come and get me."

"Where are you?"

"In school."

Russell snatched a look down the hall and saw Lenny waiting at the elevator. If it was any other time he would drop what he was doing and go and get his daughter. But the hard truth was, he could not miss this meeting. There was too much riding on it. Besides, Michele was probably just having a teenage tantrum and she'd calm down given a little time.

"Call me back on my cell phone, Michele."

"Okay. Thanks, Dad."

Russell disconnected the call and handed the phone back to Lisa.

"Everything okay, Mr. Everette?"

"Yeah," he said absently. "I'll call you."

He grabbed his things, hurried down the hallway, and boarded the elevator with Lenny.

By the time they reached the waiting limo, his cell phone rang. He slid into the car and answered the call.

"Yes, Michele. Now you want to tell me what's going on?"

"Mom is going crazy. She's all over me about everything."

"And what did you do to have your mother 'all over you'?

"Whose side are you on?"

"I'm not taking sides. I'm asking questions."

"You said we could depend on you no matter what."

"That's right. You can, within reason."

"Fine. I should have known." She disconnected the call.

Russell held the cell phone in his hand as if it could somehow answer the questions that were running around in his head. Something was wrong. How seriously remained to be seen. And there was nothing he could do about it at the moment. He'd deal with it when he returned. One thing he did know, if it had anything to do with the Parker dude, there was going to be some serious trouble.

Michele stomped away from the pay phone and looked up and down the street. She spotted Chris heading in her direction. Her heart pounded in her chest but she kept a cool expression on her face. Every female in LaGuardia High School wanted to get with Chris, but she'd caught him. They'd been seeing each other for about a month and he'd been pressing her to take their relationship to the next level. So far she'd refused, but she knew she couldn't keep him if she kept stringing him along.

"Hey, cutie," he greeted and kissed her lightly on the lips. "Why aren't you in class?" He stroked her cheek and she shivered beneath his touch.

She shrugged. "Had to make a call."

"Need to tell your mom to get you a cell phone."

"I don't want to talk about my mother," she said in a nasty tone. She rolled her eyes and pouted.

He dropped his arm around her shoulder. "Why don't you tell me all about it?" he crooned.

She looked up into his eyes and thought about how lucky she was. Chris was fine and popular. He always had money even though he didn't work and he dressed in the latest outfits every day. Chris was a catch.

Michele lowered her head and pressed closer to Chris. "Just the same old mess," she said in an offhanded way, not wanting to sound like a baby.

"Hey, then chill. What's happening later?"

"What do you mean?"

He turned her to face him. "You want to see me tonight or what?"

Her thoughts scurried around. How was she going to manage that? Her mother didn't allow her to date during the week and she had a stupid curfew of ten o'clock.

"Look, if you can't hang . . . I'll find something else to do."

"Hey, Chris," Yvonne, one of the hot mamas of the senior class, singsonged. She gave him a finger wave as she sashayed past him.

A slow smile crept across his full mouth. "Looking good, Yvonne," he called out.

Michele heard Yvonne's tinkling giggle and her insides tightened. "Don't you have any respect for me, Chris?"

"What?" he asked, the picture of innocence.

"You're looking at her like . . ."

"Like what?"

"Forget it." She shrugged his arm off her shoulder.

"You trying to tell me who I can look at and who I can talk to?" All gentleness was gone from his voice.

Michele swallowed. "No. I'm just saying that you could show me some respect. You don't have to be looking at her like that."

"You jealous?"

"I don't have anything to be jealous of. Do I?"

"Naw, as long as you take care of your man, you shouldn't have anything to worry about."

Michele forced a smile.

"So what about tonight?"

She swallowed. "I'll work it out."

"Cool, but hey, if you can't, like I said I can always find something else to do."

"I said I'd work it out," she reiterated.

Chris grinned and his right dimple flashed. "I gotta run. I'll call you tonight." He kissed her brow and headed off in the same direction as Yvonne had gone.

Michele inwardly fumed, bordering on tears or screaming, she didn't know which. First her mother, then her father, and now Chris.

She spun away and hurried toward the school building. The last thing she needed was one of her teachers getting on her for being late for class. She stole a parting glance down the street, but there was no sign of Chris. She'd have to figure out how she was going to see him.

Chapter 7

By the time her first day back at work ended, Victoria's lower back felt as if it were in a vise; her head throbbed, and her feet were beginning to swell. Was being pregnant this awful for all women or had she been specially selected to be utterly miserable?

She threw two folders of work into her lightweight leather briefcase. At any other time she would never think of bringing work home. She would have had her workload finished during her workday. But truth be told, she was exhausted. She rotated her neck and wished that she was heading to the gym instead of the shrink's office. Other women seemed to sail through their pregnancies, but not her. Was she being punished for the dark thoughts that she harbored, the fears that she refused to reveal?

Victoria sighed heavily, and slowly stood. She pressed her hand to her lower back and rubbed, hoping to relieve some of the pressure. Her private line rang. She leaned over and depressed the speaker button.

"Yes, Bridgette?"

"Your husband is here."

Of course he is, she thought miserably. "Tell him I'll be right out."

She took her trench coat from the standing rack in the corner, picked up her briefcase, and walked out to meet Phillip.

Victoria plastered a smile on her face when Phillip stood to greet her.

"Hey, sweetheart." He leaned forward to kiss her lightly on the lips. "How are you feeling?"

"Great," she lied with ease.

Phillip took her briefcase from her hand and slid his arm around her waist as he ushered her out. "Good night, Bridgette," he tossed over his shoulder as he opened the door.

"Good night, Mr. Hunter, Mrs. Hunter."

Victoria waved her good-bye.

"So how did your first day go?" Phillip asked once they were in the car.

"Fine. Just like old times." She reached for the button on the dash and turned on the radio, hoping that the music would replace conversation. She leaned back and made herself comfortable, pretending to listen to "Masquerade" by George Benson.

"He's going to be in concert in a few weeks," Phillip said. "Do you want me to get tickets?"

"I didn't think you liked George Benson."

"You like him." He turned onto Sixth Avenue and headed toward Central Park West. "That's good enough for me." He turned and briefly glanced at her, his startling dark blue eyes flashing with love.

This time Victoria's smile was gentle and sincere. "You are a wonderful man," she said and meant it.

"It's my job to be wonderful and loving and endearing," he said in a teasing voice. "I'd do whatever to see that smile of yours," he added, his tone dropping a note.

Victoria lowered her gaze and suddenly thought how appropriate the song really was. Her entire life had been set up on pretense. She pretended that she was just like everyone else, then better than everyone else. She pretended that she didn't feel the slights from her sisters, friends, and strangers about her berry-black complexion and short kinky hair. But she'd worked hard at pretending that none of that mattered, that she was above it all, that she could have what many thought she should be denied: a high-paying corporate job, a fabulous wardrobe, living in an upper-class neighborhood, and landing a white husband who obviously adored her.

"I'll pick the tickets up over the weekend. Hopefully we can get some good seats."

"Hmmm," she said absently and turned to stare out of the passenger-side window.

"If you don't want to go we don't have to, Vikki."

"I didn't say that," she snapped, suddenly irritated for no apparent reason. She folded her arms across her belly and continued to stare out the window.

Phillip drew in a breath and focused on the road and the hectic rush-hour traffic, willing himself not to get into another argument with Victoria. Lately, the least little thing set her off. He wanted to attribute it to the fluctuating hormones, but it was more than that. He knew it because he knew his wife.

Over the past few months, since the pregnancy began, Victoria was not the same woman he'd married. When they'd met, Victoria was the most vibrant, sexy, self-assured woman he'd ever encountered. It wasn't until she lay in the hospital bed that he began to realize how deep her personal demons went.

Many nights since that fateful fall down the stairs, he'd silently watched her as she slept and wondered why she had married him. Did she ever love him? He'd given up everything to be with Victoria—left his family, cast aside longtime friends, all those who pointed their fingers at them, because he loved her so very deeply. All he wanted was her love in return. He was no longer sure if he had that and he desperately wanted it back—if he ever truly had it at all.

It was his idea that they seek counseling. He felt certain that with help they could work out whatever issues they had and their marriage would be stronger for it. Although Victoria originally agreed to go to the sessions, she'd become more recalcitrant with each visit. He was trying to be patient, loving, understanding, but how much of it was he supposed to endure? Living with Victoria had turned into living with a stranger. Each time he saw her now he never knew who or what he was going to be faced with.

Phillip turned onto Seventy-Second Street a block away from Dr. Warner's office. "Talk to Regina lately?" he asked, cruising down the street looking for a parking spot.

"No. Not lately."

"We should invite her and Parker over for dinner one night soon. Or maybe we can all go out together."

"Hmmm."

Regina, Regina, Victoria mused, her thoughts darkening like an impending storm.

There was a time when it was Regina that everyone took for granted, thought of as Ms. Easygoing. And by some twist of fate, it had become Regina who demonstrated that she was the one who really had it together, that she was the one willing to sacrifice whatever was necessary to get what she wanted. Both Victoria and Toni thought that Regina was nuts for leaving Russell, for quitting a solid good-paying job as a journalist, to chuck it all and open a damned bookstore, of all things. It was Regina who was now the owner of her own business, who lived on her own with no one to answer to, who found a handsome, successful artist who adored her.

Victoria never thought she would envy Regina, but she did. Regina was comfortable in her own skin. She had her life and her head together. It was Regina who sat beside her in the hospital holding her hand and telling her that it would be all right. Hmph, what did she know? And Toni was no better, worse actually. Toni was the one who should have been doling out advice; that's what she got paid for. But Toni had no more of an idea of what to do with her own mess of a life than a pet in a classroom.

She hated when she got like this, just plain mean and evil. She tugged on her bottom lip with her teeth to keep from sobbing, something she did at the drop of a hat. Everything was fine, life was just the way she'd wanted it, until she wound up pregnant. One minute she wanted the baby like she'd never wanted anything in her life. The next, she was utterly terrified, terrified that she would birth a little black baby that looked like her. A defenseless baby that would be subjected to the feelings of no self-worth that had plagued her all her life.

Sure, black was allegedly "acceptable" now, the flavor of the month, as long as you weren't too black and your hair wasn't too nappy and your lips weren't too big or your nose too wide. All anyone had to do was look around at what was considered beautiful— it wasn't her. It was the Halle Berrys, the Vanessa Williamses, the Beyonces, and all their look-alikes that were held up in high regard.

Victoria drew in a long, sad breath as the car pulled to a stop in front of Dr. Warner's brownstone where she had her private office. Dr. Warner, hmph, blond hair and green eyes—she would never understand.

"Good to see you both," Dr. Warner said. "Please make yourselves comfortable. Can I get you anything?"

"Nothing for me," Phillip said. "What about you, sweetheart?"

"Some water," she said in a monotone.

Dr. Warner observed Victoria's closed expression and knew instantly that they were in for a tough session. Victoria had a deep-seated persecution complex. She put on a tough exterior and appeared capable of conquering anything she set her mind to. But beneath the facade, Victoria Hunter's greatest enemy was herself. She worried about her, and how her internalization of her issues were affecting her health and the health of her baby.

Dr. Warner got a bottle of water from her small refrigerator and took a glass from the overhead cabinet. She opened the bottle, filled the glass half-full, and handed both to Victoria.

"How have you been feeling, Victoria?"

"Fine."

Phillip glanced at her and reached for her hand. Victoria pulled away and folded her hands on her lap. Phillip's face flushed crimson.

"Today was your first day back to work. How was it?"

"Fine."

"I see." Dr. Warner cleared her throat and took a seat behind her desk. "Why do you dislike coming here, Victoria?"

For the first time Victoria looked directly at the doctor. "It's a waste of time. You have no idea about my life, what it's like to live my life, to be me," she spat with a vehemence that stunned Phillip and the doctor.

"Vikki," Phillip admonished.

"No, let her talk. What is it that no one understands but you, Victoria?"

Victoria's chocolate-brown eyes suddenly filled with tears and her lips trembled. "Have you ever looked in the mirror, Doctor, and hated what you saw? Did you spend the better part of your life searching for bleaching creams, praying that the next morning you'd wake up and you wouldn't be quite so black?" She sniffed back her tears. "Do you worry that any children of yours will be ridiculed, teased, and tormented because of how they look? No. I don't think so. That's why coming here is a waste of time. You don't have a clue!"

Victoria suddenly stood. "Why don't you and Phillip try to figure out what's wrong with poor Victoria, and while you're at it fix the rest of the world too?" With that she turned and stormed out.

Phillip jumped up and ran out behind her.

Victoria walked as quickly as her added weight would allow. Phillip caught up with her with ease.

"Vikki, baby." Her clasped her shoulder and spun her around, pulling her body against his.

She buried her face in his chest and sobbed. "Phillip . . ."

"It's okay," he soothed, holding her tight. "Do you have any idea how much I love you? How incredibly beautiful I think you are?"

She looked up at him through tear-filled eyes. "How could you?"

He brushed away her tears with the pads of his thumbs. "Because you are everything I want. Everything. I would be lost without you. Why won't you let me love you and allow yourself to love me back?"

"I . . . I'm so scared."

He stroked her back. "You don't have to be afraid with me, Vikki. I won't hurt you."

She sniffed again. "I want to go home," she whispered.

"Come on." He put his arm around her waist and she leaned her head against his shoulder as they walked to the car.

Victoria got in the car, strapped herself in, and closed her eyes. She wanted things to be fine; she wanted to love Phillip; she wanted to love the baby she carried, but she knew that in order to do that she had to find a way to love herself first. And she had no clue as to where to begin.

Chapter 8

Regina took a last look around the store and turned out the lights in the back. She noticed that she was running low on children's books and the self-help section was looking a bit thin. When she reached the front of the store, she made a note to have Renee review the inventory and check the catalogues for some new titles. It was always amazing to her what titles did well and which ones she had to work harder to get noticed. Romances went out of the store almost as quickly as they came in. The same thing for the new wave of urban fiction, a phenomenon that she privately hoped would quickly pass. What was beginning to gain some inroads were vampire books and horror stories written by black authors. She smiled to herself. Anne Rice and Stephen King, move over.

Regina locked the register, set the alarm, and went outside to wait for Parker. All day she'd tried to keep out of her mind what he could want to talk to her about. She checked her watch. She definitely didn't want to get in too late, especially after what Michele had pulled the night before. She locked the front door, lowered the gate, and surveyed the neighborhood.

It seemed as if each week a new business was opening in the neighborhood. When she'd first come into the area, she was very reluctant to open her business there, even though she got a great deal on the space. Ft. Greene had been notorious for robberies, drugs, and violence all during her growing-up years and that's all that she remembered. She was surprised to find this once forgotten wasteland had blossomed into a thriving oasis. Black businesses flourished, everything from antiques to African artifacts, restaurants, nightclubs, and chic boutiques. So far she was the only bookstore in the area, which was great for business, and she was thankful every day that Regina's Place continued to thrive. Especially with black bookstores across the country closing one after the other. One of her daily prayers was that a major bookstore chain wouldn't open anywhere in the vicinity.

She walked toward the corner a few feet away and leaned against the mailbox. While she waited she considered Toni's earlier visit. She felt bad for her friend, knowing how difficult it was to pull yourself up out of the hole of a failed marriage. It had taken her months after she walked out on Russell. But in Toni's case it was far worse. She'd cheated on her husband and gotten caught. Regina hoped that Toni would think with her head this time and not with her libido.

Regina peeked down the street and saw Parker's

silver Camry cruising to a stop. She waved and walked to the curb.

"Hey, baby." He leaned over and kissed her lightly on the lips.

"Hey back." She fastened her seat belt. "Where to?"

"Figured since we were downtown we could stop in Junior's for a quick bite."

"Which means I'll be forced to get a slice of cheesecake," she said, feigning being put upon. Junior's cheesecakes were nationally famous and folks came from far and wide to sample a slice.

"How awful for you." He laughed.

"It's a tough job but somebody has to do it."

"How was your day?"

"Not bad. Went by pretty quickly. Sold one of your pieces today," she said, patting him on the thigh.

"Great! Which one?"

"Blues Alley."

"Hmm." He grinned. "It's one of my favorites. I remember when I painted that. It was about five years ago when I was vacationing in New Orleans and was completely captivated by the energy, the old-world charm, and the incredible music."

"Is New Orleans as wild and crazy as they say?"

"Absolutely!" He chuckled. "We have to go sometime. You'd love it."

"Maybe during the Essence Jazz Festival," she suggested. "I've heard great things about it, and I've been dying to go for years and never get around to it."

"That's in July, right?"

"Yep."

Parker slowly nodded in thought. "We can make it a family vacation. Take the kids, hang out, and really get to know each other."

"I like it." She turned to him. "And I know the kids would love to go. You'll have to send for your daughter again. Or were you already planning on having her here for the summer, anyway?"

"That's what I want to talk to you about."

Her heart knocked, then settled. "What's wrong, Parker?"

"Let's talk inside."

Regina played the patient role for about as long as her nagging curiosity could stand it. She'd gone through the salad, two rolls, and a half glass of water. Parker talked about everything but what they'd really come there to discuss.

The waitress finally brought their meal: filet of sole, baked potato, and French-cut green beans.

"What's going on, Parker? The suspense is killing me and I know you didn't tell me we needed to meet for dinner so that we could talk about sports and the weather."

Parker took a long swallow of his iced tea and slowly put the glass down. "I got a call this morning from Lynn." He paused and looked into her eyes to gauge her reaction. Her face remained calm, although there was a thin line forming between her brows. He'd learned from the months of being with Regina that the line meant she was bracing for the worst and pretending otherwise.

He reached across the table and covered her

hand with his. "She said that I need to come and get Tracy right away and that she might be staying here for much longer than I'd originally thought."

The line grew deeper and tighter. "I don't understand. Why? What about school and—"

"Lynn . . . is ill. Very ill, from what she's telling me, and Tracy is going to need a place to stay . . . permanently."

Regina blinked several times as she processed the information. *Lynn ill . . . Tracy coming to live here for good.* "Parker, I don't know what to say. I . . . Did she . . . Lynn say what was wrong?"

He shook his head. "No. She barely told me that." He grabbed his glass and emptied the contents.

"Are you okay?" she asked gently.

"Yeah, yeah." He glanced away. "I can't remember the last time Lynn and I actually spoke before I finally found her and Tracy. I was so bitter and angry. I felt cheated and for no damned good reason. I may not have been the greatest father and husband in the world, but I did my best. Ya know? All I wanted was the opportunity to get my daughter back, make it up to her. There was a part of me that wanted Lynn to hurt as much as I did all those years. But this . . ."

"I know this isn't the way you wanted things to be, Parker. That's not the kind of man you are."

He pushed his food around on the plate with his fork. "I don't even know how to be a full-time father."

"You'll learn and you'll be good at it. Tracy is going to need you more than ever."

"She doesn't even know me."

"You'll have to change that."

He looked across the table at her. "This is going to change things between you and me for a while."

"I know. And I'll do whatever I can to help."

He sighed heavily. "Thanks."

"So . . . when are you leaving?"

"I have a flight out the day after tomorrow."

Her stomach fluttered. "Oh. How long will you be gone?"

"I'm not sure. I'll have to talk to Lynn when I get there, work things out with Tracy's school."

"You're not in this alone, Parker."

He nodded. "Kinda scary, ya know?"

"Yes, parenting is a frightening experience. You're never really sure if you get it right. It's the one course in school they never offer."

"I better get you home. I didn't mean to keep you so long."

"It's okay."

"At some point we're going to have to figure out how you and I are going to be able to spend any alone time together. I know how you feel about me spending nights at your place, but how would you feel about staying at mine—with Tracy being there?"

Regina's brows jutted upward for an instant. "Let's concentrate on getting Tracy settled and acclimated to living here. We can deal with us day by day."

The corner of his mouth curved slightly upward. "Were you always so clear-thinking and levelheaded?"

"I only wish I could say yes, but . . . it was a long struggle. I'm still getting the hang of it."

"Well, I'm definitely going to need your level head in the months to come." He signaled for the waitress, who brought the check. "How 'bout some cherry cheesecake for the road?"

"A man truly after my heart."

They laughed and headed for the cake line.

Parker pulled up in front of Regina's building. "Thanks for the company and the advice."

"Not a problem."

"Guess you better go on up."

"Why don't you come up for a few minutes? It's only nine—still early."

"Are you sure?"

"Yeah." I really thought about what you said this morning. I'm happy with our relationship and proud of it. I shouldn't have to hide that from the kids. I figure little doses at a time until they really get accustomed to seeing you around and accept the fact that you're a part of my life."

"I'd like that," he said quietly.

"Let's go."

When Regina stuck her key in the door and opened it, she was surprised to see no lights on in the living room. Her kids were notorious for watching television in the evenings until she literally chased them to bed. "Come on in."

She walked into the living room with Parker behind her and flicked on the light switch on the wall.

Her startled gasp rang in concert with the cry of her daughter, barely dressed and stretched out on the couch with Chris.

For an instant Regina was too stunned to speak, and then the words exploded in a torrent.

"Michele! What the hell is going on? Get up and

get your clothes on right now!" She whirled toward Chris. "Get out of my house. Get out."

Michele stood and covered her upper nudeness with her blouse. "Don't talk to Chris like that."

"What!" Regina was livid and breathing so hard and fast that her temples began to pound with exertion.

"Chris is my boyfriend—just like he is," she said, spitting out the word *he.*

"You are seventeen years old. This is my house and as long as you live here you will live by my rules!"

"What rules . . . sleeping around?"

Regina crossed the room in a flash and slapped Michele so hard she knocked her back down onto the couch. She stood over her daring her to move.

"I hate you!"

"Michele. Don't talk to your mother that way," Parker said in a low growl, stepping up behind Regina.

"So what are you gonna do, slap me too? You ain't my father," she screamed, sounding almost hysterical.

"Michele!"

"I may not be your father but I know an out-of-control kid when I see one."

"Parker, I think you better leave," Regina said, staring him in the eye.

Parker froze and looked at her, completely stunned.

"It's all your fault anyway," Michele railed. "If it wasn't for you, my father would be here right now. She didn't tell you that, did she?"

"Regina?"

"Please leave, Parker. This is not your problem."

He stepped back as if *he'd* been slapped and felt

the muscles of his stomach knot. "Fine. *You* handle it." He spun away and stormed out.

In all the confusion and yelling, Chris had conveniently slipped out and now mother and daughter stood face-to-face.

Chapter 9

Toni moved restlessly around her empty four-story brownstone. Everywhere she turned there were beautiful things, things that she'd put in the house in the hopes of making it a home. They should have been symbols of the success she and Charles had achieved as a couple and as a family, a far cry from the one-bedroom apartment she and Charles started out in. Instead, the artwork, the sculptures, the crystal, the imported furniture only represented an illusion of what she thought her life and her marriage were.

Walking into the living room, she went to the bar and poured herself a glass of vodka and orange juice. She rarely if ever drank—but tonight she felt as if she needed it, needed something.

She took her drink up to her bedroom and turned on the stereo. Maybe the sexy voice of the VJ Lenny Green would keep her company with his *Kissing After Dark* tunes, she thought.

Grover Washington's "Mr. Magic" was playing as

Toni kicked off her slippers and stretched out on the bed. She took a long, satisfying swallow from her glass, then set it down on the night table. She glanced at the phone and instantly thought of Alan.

How many months had she spent the night alone? She took another swallow of her drink, enjoying its warmth as the liquid slid down her throat.

Antoinette closed her eyes and leaned back against the fluffy pillows. Face it, she told herself, Charles wasn't coming back. He'd said as much and what he didn't say was apparent in his actions. She could still feel the pain of his departure as acutely as if it were yesterday. She'd practically gotten down on her knees to beg him to stay, to forgive her, to give her another chance. . . .

"Charles, please, you don't have to do this. We can work it out."

He had shoved some more clothes from his dresser drawer into a suitcase, then spun toward her. His face was twisted into a mask of unbridled anger and pain. "Work it out! What is there to work out, Toni? How can you even think that there's anything to work out between us? You slept with another man!" His breath came in short staccato bursts. "You betrayed me, our marriage, our family. And if you hadn't been caught, who knows how long it would have gone on?" He turned back to the suitcase and shoved more clothes inside.

"Charles, I love you. I'm so sorry. I can make it up to you. I swear I can."

"No, you can't, Toni," he said in a voice so low and filled with anguish that his pain truly became hers. "Your kind of love I don't need." He zipped up the suitcase.

Antoinette jumped up from the bed, seeing her life and all she'd worked for slipping away. "What about Steven?" she said, hoping to appeal to his love for their son.

"You should have thought of that before you slept with. . . ." He took a deep breath. "I really thought I could stay with you, T. There was a part of me that hoped I could get past this." He lowered his head, then looked directly at her. "But I can't. I know I can't. These past few weeks coming home, seeing you and knowing what you've done, has been killing me inside day by day. You already took away my faith and my trust. I won't let you take away what dignity I have left. I need to be able to respect myself when I look in the mirror."

Her voice trembled. "Charles . . . please think about this. Give it some time, that's all I ask. If what we had ever meant anything to you . . . please just take some time and think about it."

Charles stared at her for a long, unbearable moment. "I'll think about it. But I'm not promising anything."

The tightness in her chest eased slightly. "Thank you," she whispered.

Charles picked up his suitcase and left without another word.

Antoinette sighed heavily. That was more than two months ago. Charles had barely spoken to her since that night other than to ask about Steven. All her attempts at getting him to come over or meet at some neutral place for dinner—to talk—had been rejected. A blind man could see that he wasn't coming back, that their marriage was over. She finished her drink and went downstairs to refill her glass. By the time she polished off her third glass she'd made up her mind.

She reached for the phone and dialed Alan's number. Her heart raced like a horse set free on the range as she waited, listening to the phone ring on the other end.

Regina's words of caution leaped into Antoinette's head. She started to hang up and then she heard his voice and froze.

"Hello?"

She hesitated.

"Hello?"

"Alan . . . it's me, Toni." She squeezed her eyes shut for a moment.

"Toni, hi. I wasn't expecting to hear from you."

Antoinette cleared her throat and wished she had some more wine in her glass. "Uh . . . how are you?" she inanely asked.

"Just watching a little television."

She heard the question that hung in the air, but that Alan was too much of a gentleman to ask: *why are you calling me?*

"Oh well, if you're busy, I can always call back," she said, feeling suddenly foolish.

"Toni . . . I always have time for you. What's on your mind?"

She heard the noise from the television fade, then disappear, and realized that he actually was focusing all his attention on her—at least it sounded as if he was.

Antoinette shrugged her right shoulder as if he could see her. "I was sitting here, feeling alone, and I thought about what you said earlier." She struggled for the words that she knew once said would change the course of her life, such as it was, and Alan's too. "I was thinking that maybe if you weren't too tired or busy you might want to stop by. I, uh . . . could fix dinner, we could talk . . ."

"Are you sure that's what you want?"

She swallowed over the dryness in her throat. "Yes."

Alan was silent for a moment. "Will nine o'clock work for you?"

"Sounds fine." She released an anxious breath. "Would you like me to fix anything special?"

He chuckled lightly. "Hey, you know me, I'm easy. Whatever you want to fix is fine with me."

She smiled for the first time in hours. "Okay. So I'll see you about nine."

"Need me to bring anything?"

"No. I have everything we need. See you then."

Antoinette slowly hung up the phone. She turned and looked at the digital bedside clock. She had a little more than two hours to prepare and she wanted everything to be perfect.

Chapter 10

Regina tried to regain some semblance of control as she faced this child of hers that she no longer knew. As she stared into her brown eyes so filled with rage she wondered where her daughter had gone.

"What's all the yelling?" Darren asked from the hallway as he yawned and rubbed sleep from his eyes.

"Go back to your room, Darren."

Darren glanced from his mother to his half-dressed sister, started to ask a question, but didn't dare challenge his mother—not with the expression she had on her face.

"Now!"

Darren hurried back down the hallway to his room.

Regina focused on her daughter, who still stood there clutching her shirt. "Put your shirt on, Michele, and have a seat."

Michele grudgingly did what she was told. She

flopped down on the couch like a rag doll that had been cast aside. She defiantly folded her arms and looked away from her mother.

"What was on your mind, Michele, bringing him here?"

Michele rolled her eyes and huffed.

"I'm talking to you."

"Every time I do something it's always a problem," she spat.

"What?"

"You're on me for everything. I can't breathe."

Regina snapped her head back and forth trying to shake some sense into whatever Michele was rambling about.

"Michele, there are some basic rules that we abide by in this house and one of them is no company when I am not at home, and especially male company who winds up on my couch with you half undressed!"

Michele cut her eyes in Regina's direction. "Maybe if you were home, none of this would have happened in the first place."

"Are you telling me that this is my fault, that at the age of seventeen you still need a babysitter to make sure you do what you're supposed to do?"

"You don't care anything about me and Darren. All you're interested in is the store and Parker!"

"Michele, this is not about me and the store or Parker. This is about you and what you've done."

"That's exactly what I mean!" she shouted and jumped up. "You don't listen. You just want to blame me for everything. I can't do anything right." She whirled away and stomped off to her room, slamming the door behind her.

Regina got up too and started off after her, then

decided against it. With Michele being in that frame
of mind it was pointless to try to get her to see reason, or to come from behind the barriers she'd set
up around herself. Michele was determined to side-
step the issue at hand, but Regina also instinctively
understood that there was much more to it than
Michele bringing Chris to their home when she
wasn't there. This was an out-and-out act of rebel-
lion. Michele was trying to prove something—to her
and maybe to Chris. That scared her more than
anything. It was apparent how far Michele was willing to go. If Regina had not come home when she
did . . . She didn't want to think about it.

Suddenly exhausted, she switched off the lights
in the front of the house and headed for her bedroom. A sliver of light was coming from beneath
Michele's door. There was a time, when Michele
was a little girl, that Regina and Russell would sit
on the side of Michele's bed and alternately tell
her stories until she fell asleep.

Regina's heart felt the pangs of remembrance.
She opened her bedroom door and stepped inside.
On a tough night like this, parents sat down together
to try to figure it out. Together they worked on a
solution, showed solidarity to the kids, letting them
know that they were in it together.

But Regina had joined the ranks of the single
parents, wheeling and dealing on her own and hoping for the best. There were times when she desperately missed having someone with whom to share
the day-to-day burden of running a household and
a family. But the buck stopped with her—right or
wrong.

Regina took off her jacket and blouse and tossed

both on a side chair, then stepped out of her pants. She caught her reflection in the mirror. Not bad, she mused in an absent way. At forty, she was in good shape, probably better than she had been in her younger years. When she had left Russell, she decided to reclaim her life, and that meant reclaiming her body as well. For the first time in her life she actually had a diet and exercise plan that she stuck with. Her hair grew and her overly sensitive skin began to clear and actually look radiant.

When she looked at herself now she often wondered what is was that Russell saw when he looked at her back then and what he would see if he looked at her now. She ran her hand across her flat, taut belly. Even in the darkest days of their marriage when she saw it grinding to a halt, Russell still held her a sexual prisoner. Her body, no matter what her mind commanded, responded to his touch, the scent and feel of him. It shamed her that her body would betray her that way, even as she'd experience one shuddering orgasm after another.

Many nights when she lay alone in her bed she wondered if she'd made the right decision by leaving Russell. Maybe there was some way they could have worked out their differences. Who was she fooling? The disintegration of their marriage didn't happen overnight, and neither did her decision to leave. She had to leave to save herself. It was as simple as that.

She turned away from her reflection and took off the rest of her clothes before crawling beneath the cool sheets. There was a time when she would have gone before a firing squad before sleeping nude—even alone. But she was proud of her new body and proud of the fact that all parts were hers. This was her one little personal treat, a time when she could flaunt it.

As always before going to sleep, she reached for the phone to call Parker. As her fingers punched in the numbers she wondered what his reaction was going to be to what he'd witnessed earlier. She hated that he had to see Michele like that and what his opinion of her must be. She sighed deeply as the phone rang on the other end.

She'd find a way to explain and smooth things over. They'd talk about it and work things out. That's what couples did.

"Sorry I missed you," Parker's recorded voice said. "Please leave a message and I'll get back with you. Peace."

Regina frowned. He should have been home by now. The message tone beeped in her ear. "Hi, Parker, it's Regina. I'm so sorry about this evening. It was a nightmare. Please call me when you get in."

She checked the bedside clock. It was nearing ten. She reached for the remote and turned on the television. Maybe watching someone else's drama on her favorite show, *Law and Order,* would take her mind off her own issues momentarily.

As usual in the allotted hour, the crime was solved, the perpetrator was doing time, and the crime fighters moved on to their next case in scenes from the upcoming episode. Regina stretched and listened for any sounds coming from the house. Everything was quiet. She glanced at the clock. It was after eleven and still no word from Parker. She began to get an uneasy feeling in the pit of her stomach.

Reaching for the phone, she dialed his number again. Again she got his answering machine. Again she left him a message.

Regina leaned back against the pillows and tried to listen as the newscaster droned on about the instability in the world, and for the first time in her relationship with Parker she didn't feel as though her feet were on solid ground.

Parker listened to the tempting sounds of Regina's voice as she left the second message for the night. He started to answer when he heard her voice break over the word *please*. But the cold truth was, he didn't want to talk to Regina. He didn't want to risk what might come out of his mouth if he spoke to her right now. He'd been humiliated, not only by Regina's daughter, but by Regina. He'd come to her defense, to show Regina and Michele that he and Regina were a team. But she might as well have sucker punched him when she allowed Michele to get away with saying what she did to him. To compound the ugly, she told him to leave and that it wasn't his problem.

Hmph, maybe she was right. It wasn't his problem. And Michele was right too, he wasn't her father and never would be—not in the natural sense of the word. But he'd hoped that over time they could become a family. Now he didn't see how that was possible. It was pretty clear what Michele thought and where Regina stood. If it came down to a decision between him and her kids, he'd lose hands down.

He sat down on the couch and stretched his legs

out on the footstool. He raised the beer bottle to his lips and took a long swallow. What chance did they have? he wondered. And to complicate matters further he would soon have his daughter and her issues to deal with as well.

He loved Regina, of that he was certain, although she had yet to truly say the words to him. But for the first time he questioned the stability of their relationship and where it was going. Maybe the time away would do them both good, and when he came back they would have had time to clear their heads and see more clearly where they wanted to go. He believed there was a way to work it out, but only if Regina was willing.

Chapter 11

Toni put on dinner, checked that the flame beneath the pots was at the right height and the oven at the precise temperature. She took down two wineglasses from the overhead glass cabinet and set them on the table, then took down her best china and pale green linen napkins that matched the pattern on the dishes. She went to the antique cabinet where she kept her best silver and took out place settings for two.

After setting the table and taking a final look around she decided on the white tapers for a centerpiece. Satisfied, she hurried off to the bedroom to change the sheets, then took a quick shower.

She wanted to look attractive but not needy or too provocative, she thought as she sifted through her extensive loungewear ensembles. Finally she selected a soft pearl-gray caftan with matching harem pants that floated like air around her when she walked. She put on a hint of lipstick and her favorite body oil behind her ears and at her wrists.

The scent of her grilled salmon, garnished with her special sauce, wafted into the air. Antoinette smiled. Everything would be perfect.

Alan had never been inside her house before. She wanted everything to be just right. Checking the grandfather clock that sat in the foyer, she felt her heart beginning to race with anticipation. If nothing about Alan had changed he would be there in less than ten minutes. With that in mind, she did a room-by-room check of the three-story brownstone to ensure that everything was in its place and experienced a guilty moment of thanks that Steven had decided to stay with his father. Tonight was her night and she planned to enjoy every minute of it. She was long overdue.

Returning to the ground-floor level, she dimmed the lights and turned on the stereo to the local jazz station, CD 101.9. She was glad she'd spent the money on the state-of-the-art system. The music was as crystal-clear as if sitting live at a concert.

The front doorbell rang. Almost ten minutes exactly, she mused, delighted and giddy with excitement. Antoinette took a look in the oval mirror that hung in the foyer above the secretary, patted her hair, and wiped a small smudge of lipstick from the corner of her mouth. Tugging in a deep breath, she went to the door. She felt like a young girl expecting her first real date.

A slow smile reached her eyes and lighted her face. "Hi," she greeted.

Alan's gaze was slow and appreciative. "Hi."

She stepped aside. "Come in."

Alan walked in and tried not to act like a tourist taking in the sights.

Antoinette closed the door and came around in front of him. "We can sit in the living room." She led him inside.

"Fabulous place," he murmured, as his gaze roamed the artwork that hung on the stucco walls.

"Thanks. Have a seat. Can I get you anything to drink? Dinner will be ready soon."

"Smells great. I'll have whatever you're having."

She went to the bar and took a bottle of wine out of the ice bucket. She poured two glasses and handed one to Alan.

He raised his in a toast. "To a pleasant evening."

"To new beginnings," she responded, touching her glass to his.

Alan watched her over the rim of his glass. "You look beautiful, Toni."

Her face heated. "Thank you."

"I know you don't always walk around the house looking like that, so I can only hope that my visit inspired it."

Her smile was coy. "Perhaps." She sipped her wine, then put the glass down on the black marble table.

"I wasn't sure if you would actually come."

"Why not?"

"I guess I thought . . ."

"I meant what I said to you today. I still have deep feelings for you. I stayed out of the way not because I wanted to but because I thought it was best for you."

"I know and I appreciate it."

"So what is going on with you and your husband?"

She shifted in her seat. "Do we have to talk about that now?"

"No. But we will at some point. There's no getting around it. You understand that, don't you?"

She swallowed. "Sure. We will . . . just not right now."

Alan nodded.

"Let me check on dinner." She rose.

"I'll help you." He got up and followed her into the kitchen. "What can I do?"

Antoinette walked to the oven and pulled the door open. "You can hand me those pot holders over there on the counter."

Alan picked up the matching holders in a brilliant sunburst orange and came toward the oven. "Let me do that," he said, stepping around Antoinette to lift the baking tray out of the oven. "Where do you want this?"

"On the island counter."

Alan placed the tray on the ceramic countertop. He turned to her with a smile. "What next?"

"You can pour the wine. I thought we'd eat in the dining room. Right through there," she said, pointing toward the open archway.

"No problem."

While Alan was busy in the dining room, Antoinette took out the serving bowls and filled them with the sautéed vegetables and wild rice. She placed both on a wooden tray.

For the first time in months she actually felt light, happy almost, she thought, listening to Alan hum offbeat to the music. It was a feeling she wasn't certain she'd ever feel again. She liked it and she was going to work really hard to keep it.

"Dinner is wonderful," Alan complimented, forking a piece of salmon into his mouth. "Do you always cook like this?"

"I actually like to cook," she admitted. "My husband and son didn't really care one way or the other as long as it was a lot of it and hot." She laughed, but there was no joy in the sound.

"How are you, Toni, really? And please don't insult my intelligence by telling me you're fine."

She glanced at him, then down at her plate. She put down her fork and picked up her glass of wine. How could she explain? she wondered. What could she safely tell him without him feeling either empathy or disgust?

"I've been trying to take one day at a time."

"How is Steven?"

"If I didn't know better, I'd think he hated me. I haven't told him what happened—not exactly. But not having his father here is enough. He barely speaks to me unless he needs something. It's almost a relief when he's not here."

"I'm sorry."

"Yeah, so am I." She picked up her wineglass, changed her mind, and put it back down. "There was a time when I had such great hopes for my marriage and my life with Charles. Not a day goes by that I wonder what went so terribly wrong." She glanced around at her elegant space. "I was foolish enough to think that if I made everything beautiful, our life would be beautiful, too."

"There's no way to predict how any marriage is going to turn out, no matter what good intentions you may have. I'm a prime example. I never thought my marriage would end either."

Antoinette briefly recalled the counseling sessions with Alan while he dealt with the dissolution of his own marriage and the pain and uncertainty it caused him. And now here she was being counseled by her former client.

"It's funny, sometimes I think that I'm somehow being punished for what happened between me and you."

"Why would you say that?"

"What I was searching for with you I should have been looking for at home. I didn't do that. I let my heart think for me and I did something not only morally wrong, but ethically as well."

"Do you regret our time together, Antoinette?" he asked, looking straight into her eyes.

"No. I don't. They were some of the most happy, fulfilling times of my life."

"Mine too."

The sexy strains of Najee's sax floated through the air.

Alan reached across the table and took her hand. "I want us to try again, Toni. I miss you. I miss the way we were with each other. These last few months away from you have been hell. I admit that."

Antoinette briefly glanced away, torn between what was being offered and what she might have to leave behind forever.

"I've missed you too." She eased her hand out of his light grasp and stood. "Wanna help me?" She picked up her empty plate and wineglass.

"Sure." Alan followed suit.

With the dishes in the dishwasher and the pots and trays put away, Antoinette took Alan's hand and went into the living room.

"Can I get you anything?" she asked.

"No, I'm fine." He patted the space beside him on the love seat. "But you can come and sit with me for a few minutes."

Antoinette smiled and sat beside him, relishing in the warmth of his body next to hers, something that had been absent from her life for months— the warmth and comfort of a man. Alan put his arm around her shoulder and drew her close. She rested her head against his chest and was soothed by the rhythmic beating of his heart.

They sat together not speaking, but enjoying the music, the atmosphere, and getting reacquainted with being in each other's company again.

Alan gently stroked her hair, letting it slide between his fingers. It was taking all of his self-control not to kiss her, caress her, make love to her the way he'd been dreaming of all these weeks. He'd never imagined feeling this way again about anyone. When Antoinette had told him that her husband knew about them, there was a part of him that ached for her and what she was going through, but there was also a part of him that was relieved. He'd never wanted to be "the other man." But he also understood that what they were doing was wrong and no good could ever come of it.

His finger grazed her jaw and her soft murmur shot straight to his loins and began to throb. She turned toward him in his arms and looked up into his eyes just the way he remembered. Slowly he lowered his head until his lips met hers.

Her mouth seemed to melt against his as her lips slowly parted to welcome the sensation of his tongue. Like a dance that was all too familiar, they moved in sync with each other as if time and circumstance had not separated them.

"I've missed you," Alan murmured in her ear while his hands ran over the length of her body. "More than you can imagine." He eased her back against the couch as his hand massaged the insides of her thighs.

Antoinette shuddered slightly. "So have I."

Alan opened her top, exposing her warm brown skin, and placed hot, tiny kisses along her collarbone until she moaned with pleasure. He pushed up her bra to sample the swell of her breasts.

Antoinette squeezed her eyes shut as ripples of pleasure rolled through her from her head to her toes. She reached for him, no longer willing to be denied the release she so desperately sought. And like two adolescents they scrambled out of their clothing, tossing them carelessly to the floor, having only one thing in mind—each other, only at the last minute remembering protection.

The instant Antoinette felt Alan enter her, it was as if she'd somehow escaped the life she lived day to day and was transported to a realm of pure pleasure. The fit, the moves, the touches, the whispers were all perfect, better than she remembered. She wanted to show him how much she missed him, how much she enjoyed what he was doing to her body, and she did, wrapping her legs around his waist to capture his every move.

Alan groaned, clasped her hips to pull her closer, needing to bury himself within her warmth, take away the empty coldness that had taken residence in his heart since he had been without her. "I love you," he whispered.

Antoinette heard the words, wrapped them close to her as her body vibrated in release. She buried her head in his shoulder and silently wept.

"Have you spoken with Charles?" Alan asked later as they lay wrapped in each other's arms.

Antoinette's heart knocked in her chest. "No. Not really."

Alan was quiet for a moment. "I need you to answer me honestly."

"All right."

"If Charles decided he wanted to work things out, would you consider it?"

It was a question that plagued her. She still loved Charles, and there was a part of her that always would. He was the father of her child and he'd never been anything but good to her. But would she open the doors to her heart if he decided he wanted to try again?

"Honestly, Alan, I . . . don't know."

He nodded his head. Slowly he eased out of her hold and sat up. He reached for his discarded clothing, stood, and began to get dressed. "I was hoping you wouldn't say that," he said in a strained voice. "But I kind of expected it." He stepped into his shorts, then his pants, and turned to her. "So what was tonight really about, Toni?"

She sat up and, feeling suddenly naked, grabbed

her top and covered herself. "I don't know what you mean."

"I think you do." He sat down beside her. "I know how I feel about you. I know what I want. But I don't think you do, not really."

She lowered her gaze and focused on her hands.

Alan put on his socks and shoes. "I knew when we started out that it wasn't right, but I was drawn to you in a way that I couldn't get around. The time away from you helped me to realize some things." He angled his body to look at her. "I can't, nor will I attempt to, play second to your husband. That's not who I am. If we're going to be together, it has to be right. You need to clean your plate and decide what you want once and for all." He stood and buttoned his shirt. "Until that happens, I'm not going to be the one you call when you feel like having sex without a commitment."

"Alan—"

"No, it's cool. Really. I want to put my cards on the table. Tonight was great. I want more of this on a permanent basis. It's as simple as that. The rest is up to you."

He leaned down and kissed her lightly on the lips. "Good night, Toni."

Antoinette sat immobile as she watched Alan walk out the door. She knew he was right. The fact was, she was torn. There remained the lingering hope that Charles would come back to her. And on the flip side she wanted Alan, too.

She gathered up her clothes and went upstairs, still feeling the tingle between her legs as she walked. Standing under the pulsing beat of the shower, she let Alan's words and the cleansing waters wash over her. She had to make a decision. But for the moment, she simply wanted to savor the night in case it was the last one that they shared.

Chapter 12

Phillip helped Victoria out of the car and up the stairs into the house. She'd been silent for the entire ride home and he wondered what was running through that head of hers. He supposed what baffled him most was Victoria's strong lack of self-esteem. It was a concept he couldn't seem to grasp. Victoria was an incredible woman. One any woman with sense would envy. But she was totally trapped by her visions of herself and what she believed others thought of her.

From the beginning, his family and friends had warned him that a mixed union was only asking for trouble. He disregarded all the naysayers, so much so that he'd been ostracized from his own family as a result. He firmly believed that the difficulties would come from outside their marriage, but together they could battle anything. It never occurred to him in his wildest imaginings that the biggest obstacle to their happiness would be his wife.

With a heavy heart he hung up his jacket and watched silently as Victoria took one stair at a time to their upper-floor bedroom. How could he help her? How could he make her see her own value to him and to the world? It was imperative that he do so for her sake, his, and their baby's, because in the recesses of his heart, if he could not find a way to reach through the barriers that Victoria had set up around her heart, he didn't know how he would be able to stay in the marriage—a fact that pained him more than anything.

Phillip went into the kitchen and put on a kettle for some tea. He knew how much Victoria loved a cup of hot tea before bed. While he waited for the water to boil, he came to a decision. What little he did know about human nature and the type of person everyone ultimately becomes was that the foundation begins in the home. He'd never met Victoria's family, and in all the years they'd been together she'd spoken little about them, if at all. As with his family, none of them were at their wedding and they didn't exchange cards or phone calls during holidays or birthdays. He knew where he stood with his family and he'd come to live with that. But in the back of his mind, he firmly believed that Victoria's family was at the root of her issues.

The kettle whistled shrilly, snapping him from his musings. He was going to get to the bottom of it, he decided as he poured the boiling water into a ceramic mug over the chamomile tea bag. He squeezed a lemon into the water and added a pinch of sugar.

Phillip placed the mug and some unsalted crackers onto a tray and headed up to their bedroom. He wasn't sure where he would start looking for Victoria's family, but he was determined to find them and make them answer for what he believed they'd done to her.

This was his wife, he thought as he handed her the tea and looked down into her sad eyes. He loved her with all of his heart and could not bear to see her hurt or suffering. Whatever it took to make it right, he was willing to do—and he would.

"Thank you," she whispered, setting the tray on her lap. She gave him a crooked smile. "You're always so thoughtful."

He stroked her cheek. "With you it's easy. Don't you know that by now?"

She lowered her head. "I don't mean to be so . . . miserable and unhappy. I don't mean to take my frustrations out on you. Really, I don't. It's just . . . sometimes I feel so inadequate, less than."

"But why, baby? Tell me why so that I can understand. It's more than you being dark. I know that. You have too much going on for you to fall into that."

"That's what you don't understand, Phillip. My skin is who I am, how I'm defined. When you walk into any room in the world, no one is going to say, What is that white man doing here? or question your right to rise to any level you want. It's all part of the white entitlement." She saw him flinch but continued. "I can't do that. I never could. If I achieve some goal, it must be because I've gotten some preferential treatment. If I walk into an expensive boutique, I get followed around the store or shown to the discount section. It doesn't matter that I have a platinum American Express card in my wallet, and probably make more money in a year than all the employees put together. And what makes it worse is that it not only comes from whites, it comes from our own people. You can't simply be pretty, you have to be a pretty black girl. And within our own culture there are levels of pretty, of who we put in front of the camera or push out in front to represent us." She shook her head sadly. "Not much has changed in four hundred years." She looked into his blue eyes. "I endured that kind of ridicule all my life. I don't want that for our child. I don't."

Phillip felt suddenly beaten, as if he were in a race that he could never win. It was true he could not change the world alone. But he could work at trying to change the perceptions of what went on in his own home. There was no way that their child could battle the elements of a twisted society if their child's own mother had such a dim view of herself. Victoria needed to be strong and whole inside so that their child would be as well. He knew he could not teach their son or daughter what it meant to black in America. That must come from Victoria. But in order for her to do that, in order to pass that on, she needed to come to grips with who she was and her value to herself and the world. And until he could uncover the deep roots of her self-hatred they didn't stand a chance.

Phillip leaned over and kissed her forehead. "Try to get some sleep. I'm going to work a little bit downstairs in the office."

"All right."

"If you need anything call me."

"I will."

Phillip went down to the home office, turned on the lights, and placed a phone call to a friend of his. He had to start somewhere.

Chapter 13

Regina was reading the newspaper at the kitchen table when Michele came in. She looked up and immediately caught the sullen expression on Michele's face.

"Good morning, Michele."

Michele walked to the refrigerator and pulled it open. She took out the container of orange juice.

"'Mornin'," she said, barely opening her mouth.

Regina swallowed. "Have a seat."

Michele tossed her backpack into an available chair and plopped down into another.

"I hope you've had time to think about what transpired last night, Michele."

Michele glanced away, but at least had the decency to look embarrassed.

"You know that what you did was perfectly unacceptable under any circumstances."

Michele pressed her lips together but didn't speak. She focused on the photograph of her brother tossing a basketball that was Scotch-taped to the fridge.

"You have six months before you graduate. You have plans for college and for a life. I don't want to see everything that you've worked for and dreamed about come to a halt because you have some idea in your head of proving something to me or getting back at me for whatever infraction you have in your head that I've committed." She paused a moment. "Have you had sex with Chris?"

Michele's gaze flashed in surprise and landed for a moment on her mother's face before darting away. "No," she murmured.

A mild wave of relief loosened the knot in Regina's stomach. "Do you plan to?"

"Ma . . . what kind of question is that?"

"The kind of question that apparently needs to be asked."

Michele shifted her body in the chair. Her bottom lip trembled for a moment. "I don't know." She blinked rapidly as if fighting a bout of impending tears.

Regina wanted to get up and wrap her arms around her, soothe her, and make right whatever was wrong, but she knew she must stand her ground. Michele didn't need pampering, she needed a reality check. Regina leaned forward and braced her arms on the table.

"Listen to me, Michele, whatever you may think of me is totally unimportant. This is about you and your life and the choices that *you* make. I understand the changes that your body is going through. We all go through them. I understand your attraction to Chris. But at the same time I understand that a wrong turn in your life now cannot be al-

tered. Having sex with someone is a sacred thing.
At least it should be. It should not be done to show
Chris anything, or me for that matter. You have
nothing to prove." She took a breath. "I know I
can't stop you if that's what's in your heart to do.
But there is more at stake than pregnancy. When
you have sex with anyone, you are putting your life
in their hands as well as your heart. I don't want to
see anything happen to you. All I ask is that you
wait—if you can—and be sure that it's what you really want and for the right reason—that you love
him. And to be truthful, at seventeen you really don't
know what real love is. By the time you're twenty
you'll feel the same way about someone else. Then
what?"

"Do you love Parker?" She stared her mother in
the eyes.

"Yes," Regina said without hesitation and surprised herself with the relief she felt at finally ad-
mitting it out loud. "Yes, I do."

"What about Dad? You loved him, right?"

"Yes, I did. But I wasn't seventeen years old
when I slept with him either."

Michele bit down on her lip and looked away.

"As I said, Michele, the choice is yours. Whatever
decision you make you will have to live with. All I
ask is that you protect yourself at all times, no matter what Chris wants. Do you understand what I'm
telling you?"

Michele nodded.

"I guess you also know that you can forget about
going anywhere for the next two weeks, no calls,
no company, no anything."

"Ma!"

"There's nothing to discuss, Michele. You need

some time to think, and two weeks will help with the process. Now, go on and get ready for school before you're late for class."

Michele pulled herself up from the table and grabbed her backpack. She looked at her mother. "How do you know when you're in love?"

Regina smiled gently. It was an age-old question that people were still trying to answer. "Being in love is a tricky thing. Many times our bodies tell us it's love but it's only lust. How do you know?" She blew out a breath. "When you can see yourself in the future with that person. When you know that you want to grow and share with that person. When you can finish their thoughts and they can finish yours. When the only thing that matters is seeing them happy and knowing that they want the same thing for you." She smiled up at her daughter. "And that's just for starters."

Michele hugged her backpack to her chest. "Thanks."

"Anytime."

While she sipped her coffee, Regina watched her daughter leave. She had no idea if what she said would stick with Michele. The heart and body were treacherous things and didn't always work in concert with each other. All she could hope for was that she'd given Michele some things to think about and that the foundation of values she'd built and set for her daughter would kick in when Michele needed them most; that and a whole lot of praying.

Regina got up from the table and put her cup in the sink. Generally she opened the bookstore at ten. She checked the clock above the fridge. It was seven-thirty. She had yet to hear from Parker. That worried her. She knew he had a class to teach at eleven, so he should still be home. But the question remained, if he was home why had he not returned her calls?

She hurried into her bedroom, got her purse and a lightweight jacket, and headed out moments after Michele and Darren.

If he wouldn't return her phone calls, she thought as she got behind the wheel of her Toyota, he'd have no choice but to deal with her face-to-face. Barring any major traffic jams on the Brooklyn Bridge, she could be in Lower Manhattan in thirty minutes.

The guesstimated thirty-minute drive turned into a horrific hour of stop-and-go traffic as all motorists were rerouted, stopped, and searched because the president was in town. Streets were blocked off and traffic lines went on for miles on the alternate routes through the city. In any other town, Regina thought, battling her growing ire, it would be a cause for celebration when the president of the United States came to visit. But in a bustling, traffic-driven city like New York it was a major pain in the neck.

By the time she pulled up in front of Parker's loft, she was so drained she just wanted to put her head down on the steering wheel and take a nap. She'd been a heartbeat away from morphing into one of those irate drivers that developed a major case of road rage. She glanced up at the building, hoping to see some movement behind the windows. She saw none. The way her luck had been going so far, he probably wasn't home.

Regina turned off the car, got out, and set the alarm before walking across the street to Parker's building. She pressed the bell and crossed her fingers.

"Who?" came Parker's voice through the intercom.

"It's me, Regina."

She waited for a moment, then two, then three before the buzzer finally sounded and released the lock on the door. She took the freight elevator up to his floor. The elevator ride always reminded her of the movie *Fatal Attraction* when Michael Douglas and Glenn Close got it on. She got off and walked down the narrow corridor to his front door. For a moment she hesitated before ringing the bell, wondering for the first time what she was going to say. She finally raised her hand to ring the bell when the door was pulled open.

Parker stood in front of her, his face still a bit dreamy with sleep. His shirt was fully open, exposing his chest, and his drawstring cotton pants hung low on his narrow hips. Regina fought to keep her gaze focused above his waist.

"Hi," she said softly.

"Come in." He stepped aside to let her pass.

"I tried to call you," she said, turning to face him as he closed the door.

"I got your messages." He led her into the front room.

"Why didn't you call me back?" she asked, putting her purse down on the black futon.

"Thought it was best that I didn't. I wasn't in a very good frame of mind."

"I'm sorry about last night. Sorry you had to get dragged into that kind of drama."

Parker crossed the room and sprawled out in a lounge chair. "Like you said, Gina, it's not my problem." He ran his hand across his face. "So, what brings you here?"

Regina's blood ran cold. She'd never seen Parker like this—so distant as if they were strangers.

"I wanted to apologize for one thing."

"Uh-huh. And the other thing?"

"I was hoping that we could talk."

"About what?"

"What is wrong with you?" she asked suddenly.

"You're kidding me, right?"

"No, I'm not. What is the problem?"

Parker got up. "You want some coffee, juice?"

"No. But I would like an answer."

He moved to the other side of the enormous space that served as the kitchen and looked at her from the opposite side of the counter.

"What do you want me to say, Regina, that everything is cool, that I don't have a problem with what went down last night? Because if you do, then we have more of a problem than I thought."

"What are you telling me?"

"I'm telling you that I got your message loud and clear. Your kids are your business. I'm not their father. And you can handle *your* stuff by *yourself.*"

Regina's heart was suddenly beating so fast she could hardly breathe. "So you're saying it's over?" she asked incredulously.

He braced his palms on the counter. "I'm saying that I can't, nor will I, compete with your children. When I heard Michele talking to you the way she did, the first thing that came into my mind was that I wanted to protect you, let you know that I had your back, and let her know that I wouldn't stand idly by and watch her disrespect you. Funny thing is, you don't seem to feel the same way, and I don't see how we can have a relationship if that's the way you feel and that's the way I'll be treated when it's 'family matters.' "

"Parker, that's not how I meant for it to sound or for you to take it that way."

"Well, it did and I did." He looked at her for a moment. "Look, I've got to get ready for class. I have a long day and I'm leaving in the morning."

Regina got up. "You have this all wrong."

He didn't respond.

She picked up her purse and walked to the door. "We'll talk when I get back."

She glanced at him over her shoulder. "Sure. Have a safe trip." She walked out and slammed the door behind her.

Parker stood in the center of the room, coffee cup in hand. It had taken all his willpower not to take Regina in his arms, hold her, kiss her, drag her off to his bedroom. But he knew that would be a mistake. He knew coming into this relationship that it wouldn't be easy dealing with a woman and children—half-grown children at that. But he hung in there because he wanted Regina in his life more than he wanted anything.

Last night he'd been thrown for a loop. He was still emotionally reeling from what happened. He loved Regina. But last night showed him a side of her he'd never confronted before, and now he needed to decide if he wanted to stay along for the ride or move on without her.

He turned away from the door and walked to his bedroom, the questions and uncertainty weighing heavy on his heart.

* * *

For several long moments Regina sat immobile behind the wheel of her car. How could things have disintegrated so quickly? She was still hard-pressed to come to grips with what Parker's issue was. Yes, she agreed, Michele was rude, she shouldn't have said what she did. As for her, she was so startled and embarrassed for herself and for her daughter that the only thing she could think of was to tell Parker to go.

She supposed she carried around this silly notion that she wanted Parker to see her little family only in a good light, that she'd done a great job as a single mom, that she had wonderful kids and her house was totally in order. It mattered to her what Parker thought. She chuckled silently. *Old bad habits die hard,* she thought. She'd been trapped in that stifling philosophy most of her life. All she wanted to do was please everyone, make everyone happy even at the expense of her own happiness. It was important to her how other people thought of her, because at times she'd thought so little of herself.

She'd overcome most of it. Not without a major life upheaval, but she'd done it and rocked a few boats in the process. However, some of the old demons still lingered and they had reared their ugly heads last night.

Regina glanced up at Parker's window and saw him moving about. However, one troubling element did remain: was she truly willing to allow Parker deep enough into her life so that they could continue to raise their children together—as a team with one mind and heart?

She'd fought for her independence. She'd struggled against powerful odds to pull away from the vines that bound her to her husband, a job, her friends, even her mother. But she'd done it. She'd struck out on her own when everyone else believed she'd fall flat on her face. Every day was still a battle to prove them wrong. But she'd secured her freedom. She'd finally reached that point in her life where the only person she answered to was herself. She knew she could handle on her own what life dished out to her, and she fiercely held on to that independent lifestyle.

She turned the key in the ignition, looked for traffic, and pulled out. Was she willing to let part of that autonomy go and share her life, her family with someone else again?

The question dogged her all the way back to Brooklyn.

Chapter 14

Regina inched her way through the morning rush-hour traffic, still shaken by what had transpired between her and Parker. She tried to understand his side of the issue, but he failed to see hers.

They were at a crossroads, a definite turning point in their relationship, and they both needed to decide if it was what they wanted and how they could make it work.

She pulled up in front of Regina's Place and luckily was able to find a parking space without too much trouble. She gathered up her things, set the car alarm, and walked toward the store. After deactivating the store alarm and opening the gates she went in and began her day. As she flicked on the lights, turned on the computer, and got the coffee going she hoped that the day would remain busy enough so that she could keep her mind off of her own issues for a while.

No sooner had she had her first cup of coffee than Toni called.

"I don't want you to preach at me," Toni said instead of hello.

Regina took a seat because she knew it was going to be a story that would take a minute. She pulled her coffee mug closer and took a sip. "I'm listening."

"Well, last night Alan came over."

Regina shook her head because she knew what was coming next. "So how was it?" she asked, skipping any preliminaries. She could almost see that coy smile of Antoinette's over the phone line.

"As wonderful as always."

"Glad to hear it, but there must be more to it for you to call. I know you don't want to give me some blow-by-blow."

"No! Girl, please."

"So . . . what's up, really?"

Antoinette sighed. "After it was over he asked me, if Charles came back, what would I do?"

"What did you tell him?"

"I told him I didn't know."

Regina tsked. "If you didn't know, Toni, why did you have Alan over there in the first damned place? I suppose he felt like a two-dollar hooker on a booty call after that."

"Damn, Regina, you didn't have to say that. It's not the way it was."

"Then how was it? And be honest with yourself for a minute. You used Alan to get yours. You used a man who you knew cared about you and wouldn't say no. You're doing to him the same thing you did to Charles."

"Whose side are you on, anyway? You're supposed to be my friend."

"I am your friend. If I wasn't, I would shut my mouth and let you keep making the same mistakes over and over." Regina took a breath. "No one wants to feel used or like they are unimportant in your life, that they only fill a need when you want it filled."

"That's not the way it was," Toni said with less vehemence and conviction.

"Don't convince me, convince yourself, Toni."

The bell over the door chimed. Regina looked up at Russell.

"Listen, I need to go. I'll call you tonight."

"Sure." Antoinette hung up.

Regina replaced the phone on the cradle and swiveled her chair to meet Russell's entrance. He never just dropped in to say hello. His visits were usually the prelude to some problem. Whatever it was she'd deal with it. She lifted her coffee mug to her lips and drained the contents.

"A little early even for you, Russ."

"I want to talk to you."

She arched a sarcastic brow. "Really? And I thought you stopped in for some books."

His jaw clenched as he looked at the woman who was once his wife, the woman who bore his children and seemed very content in the role. Ever since the years of their divorce he was still getting accustomed to this in-your-face, independent Regina. And as much as her new attitude ticked him off, it turned him on at the same time.

He cleared his throat, took off his trench coat, and tossed it across the checkout counter. Regina rolled her eyes, but held her tongue.

"I was on my way to D.C. yesterday and I got a call from Michele."

Her stomach fluttered for a moment. "Was something wrong?"

"That's what I want to find out from you. She says she wants to move out and live with me."

Regina felt as if she'd been slapped by some unseen source. "She said what?" She couldn't believe Michele had gone that far, but if last night was any indication of the direction their daughter was taking, then anything was possible. It was bad enough that Michele called her father when she'd spent the night with Parker, then the "I want to leave home" call, and the incident last night. Regina let out a ragged breath.

"I don't know what's going on with Michele lately," Regina admitted reluctantly.

"Well, something must not be right if she wants to leave, Regina. And I want to know what it is. Is that friend of yours bothering her, 'cause so help me—"

"Of course not! I barely have Parker at the house."

"That's right, you opt for spending the night out and leaving Michele and Darren alone."

"That's not fair, Russell. I have a life too, as I'm sure you do. But you don't see me sitting up in your kitchen when you come in."

"I don't have the responsibility of children in my house either."

"Well, if you're so concerned, then spend some more time with them instead of just sending money and making phone calls." She flipped her hand in the air as she spoke. "Let them stay at your house on the weekends, during the holidays and school breaks."

For a moment Russell was flustered. The last

thing he expected was for Regina to toss the ball in his lap. What would he do with two teenagers in his house? How would that affect his life? It had been years since he'd lived with them, and he really didn't know them that way anymore. And suddenly that realization saddened him. All the years, the time and shared experiences that he'd missed out on or didn't take part in when it came to his kids. He looked into Regina's steady gaze, saw all the history there, the good and bad times. Damn it, he was still in love with her, maybe more so now than before. He glanced away to regain his balance.

"Fine," he said, rising to the challenge. "I'll come and pick them up on Friday." He reached for his coat and draped it over his arms.

Regina blinked several times. "I'll tell them."

"Good, I'll stop by after work, around seven."

Regina nodded.

His gaze ran over her for a moment. "Talk to you later."

"Sure," she murmured as she watched him walk out. Russell never did anything without a reason, and she wondered what his real reason was now.

She got up from behind the desk and headed to the back. She needed to review the inventory and put a new order in or at least get it started and let her assistant Renee finish it up when she arrived.

As she combed the bookshelves and compared it with the new catalogue she'd just received, the bell over the door chimed again. She put down her paperwork and walked to the front of the store.

"Parker."

"Hey, Gina." He slung his hands in his jacket pocket.

"Don't you have a class?"

"I have someone taking over for me." He stepped closer to her. "I wanted to talk to you and I didn't want it to wait until I got back."

Regina swallowed over the sudden dryness in her throat. "Okay." She folded her arms and waited.

"Look, I don't like what happened last night. For some reason that I still can't grasp, it really bothered me. But what bothered me more was this morning." He glanced down for a moment, then looked directly at her. "I don't want to fight with you, Gina. I want this thing between us to work and I certainly don't want our kids being the reasons why it can't. You're important to me."

Regina stepped closer. "You're important to me too, Parker. I can't tell you how sorry I am. I didn't mean to dismiss you or your concerns." She took a breath. "It's been a real struggle for me to get to where I am now, emotionally and mentally. I think you know that."

He nodded.

"And I think I just had a major bout of 'I can do this alone.' I was thinking really hard on the ride back from your place. I know what my issues are and I'm going to work on them. All I ask is that you be patient with me."

"All I ask is that you let me be a part of your life, Gina. I don't want to feel like the outsider. I want to make a life with you. I think you know that. But in order for that to happen you have to be willing to cross that invisible line you've set up around yourself. I'm not Russell."

"I know that."

He stepped closer, forcing her to look up at him. "Truce?" He lifted her chin with the tip of his finger.

A slow smile played across her mouth. "Truce."

"You have no idea how badly I want you right now," he said in a voice so deep and throbbing that she felt it in the center of her chest.

"Tell me," she whispered an instant before his warm lips covered hers.

He wrapped his arms around her and pulled her close, letting her feel exactly what he meant. She moaned softly against his mouth as he pulled her hips to meet the erection that beat with a life of its own.

Reluctantly he pulled away. "I'm leaving in the morning," he said, letting his eyes trail over her face. "I want to see you before I go. All of you."

She remembered her lecture to Toni about letting her body rule her head. She knew she needed to be home, especially tonight, but she also knew that she needed to be with Parker as well.

"I'll close early, come by your place for a couple of hours."

"I'll fix dinner."

"I can't stay."

"I know." He kissed her again, long, lazy, and slow. "I'll have you home by eight."

"I'll be there by four."

"I'll be waiting. I better go before neither of us makes it out of here."

She giggled. "Yeah, I think you're right. See you later."

He kissed the tip of her nose. "Later."

Regina leaned up against the counter savoring the taste of Parker on her lips and the feel of his sex between her thighs. Much as she hated to admit it, Toni had a point.

She let out a breath. Well, if she wanted to be out of there by four she had better get busy. She returned to the back of the store and continued with her inventory. It was barely noon and her day had been action-packed already, she thought. If the early morning events were any indication of the excitement in store for her later, she was truly going to have her hands full.

Maybe she would have a chance to run downtown to her favorite lingerie shop and pick up something really special for her rendezvous with Parker. She wanted him to keep her on his mind during his trip. She smiled as another idea hit her.

She turned down one of the aisles and searched the shelves for the book *Expressing Your Inner Sensuality* that had recently arrived. Locating it, she pulled it down from the shelves and went to the front. Taking a seat behind the counter, she flipped the book open and began to read.

With a couple of hours to spare she figured she could absorb a thing or two and perhaps have some real surprises in store for Parker.

Phillip walked into the office of his longtime friend Mike Nichols, a former detective with the NYPD, now running his own PI firm.

"Phil." Mike stood, his burly physique making Phillip's six-foot stature seem miniscule by comparison. He extended his mitt of a hand.

"Thanks for seeing me, Mike." He shook his friend's hand and took a seat.

"Anything for a buddy. What's up? What can I do for you?"

"I want you to investigate the background of my wife."

Chapter 15

"Renee, I'm going to be leaving early today," Regina said.

"Everything okay?"

"Yes, I just have some errands to run. So I'll need you to close up."

"No problem."

"I started the inventory." She handed Renee the order form. "Finish what you can and I'll put the order in tomorrow."

"Sure." Renee looked over the list. "We need to order greeting cards, too."

"Right. Add those to the list as well."

"Will Mr. Heywood be delivering any new prints? I have some orders for the ones we have here."

"I'll find out."

"You're so lucky."

Regina tilted her head to the side. "Lucky?"

"Yeah." Renee leaned on the counter. "You have a great business, your kids are cool, and you have a fine man." She laughed.

"I guess I do have it kinda good," Regina quipped. "But it didn't all come easy."

"What do you mean?"

"I had to make a lot of changes in my life to get where I am."

"Like what?"

Regina patted Renee's shoulder. "Long story. Maybe when we have some quiet time I'll tell you all about it."

"I'd really like to hear about it. I want to be where you are one day in my life," she confessed.

"Why?"

She smiled. "Long story. Maybe when we have some quiet time I'll tell you all about it."

They laughed.

"It's a date." Regina picked up her purse. "See you tomorrow."

Regina took the ten-minute ride to downtown Brooklyn from her store, parked in the municipal parking lot, then hustled over to Brown Sugar, the lingerie shop.

"Hi, I'm Kelly. Can I help you?" the cheery sales clerk asked.

"Hmm. I think I'll just look. Thanks."

"If you need anything let me know."

Kelly watched Regina as she strolled through the store flipping through the rows of lingerie. She always tried to observe the customers when they came in, what made them stop and look twice or pick up one item over the other. It helped her gauge what they were into and what she could get them to buy. This one seemed to have a thing for sheer black. Conservative.

Regina wandered through the aisles looking for the perfect sexy outfit. She noticed a sheer black teddy with a matching thong. She lifted the outfit from the rack and held it out in front of her.

"That would look great on you," Kelly said, easing up alongside her.

Regina laughed self-consciously. "Thanks."

"But with your complexion and those light brown eyes, why don't you try something a bit more daring?"

"Daring?"

Kelly gave her a wicked smile and crooked her finger for Regina to follow her. She walked across the store to a rack in the rear. She searched through the row and pulled out what looked like a body shaper, but it was totally sheer in a cinnamon brown that was identical to Regina's complexion. It had a floral design that covered each breast and a cutout in the center.

She held it up for Regina. "With this number it looks like you have nothing on at all but two flowers." She winked at Regina. "This will make his eyes pop. I have one just like it. Drove the man crazy." She giggled.

Regina held it up trying to imagine herself in it and what Parker's reaction would be when he saw her.

"What does he like?" Kelly asked, noticing Regina's hesitation.

Regina shrugged slightly, realizing that she'd never thought much about it. "Not sure, to tell you the truth."

"Well, this will get you started." She looked Regina up and down. "I'd say you are about a thirty-six B?"

Regina nodded, feeling her face flush.

"Come with me. I have something that will knock him out."

She went behind he counter and pulled out a box of demi bras in an assortment of designs and colors, with matching panties or thongs.

"I know when I put these on, my man's eyes bulge." She leaned across the counter and lowered her voice in a sister-girl tone. "When we met at some stuffy function or the other, he was this real straitlaced guy, not a kink in him, if you know what I mean." She giggled, then continued. "Anyway, we get to talking and he tells me all about his divorce, that he really doesn't date much. I felt kinda sorry for him, ya know? So we talk some more and decide we'd like to see each other again. The thing was, I really dug the guy, totally not my usual type, but there was something about him." She shook her head. "Anyway, I figure, when I do get the chance to lay it on him I planned to make it a night he wouldn't forget. But guess what?"

"What?" Regina asked, totally engrossed in the story.

"He must have been thinking the same thing, 'cause, sister, let me tell you I walked around in a daze for almost a week." She laughed and slapped her palm on the counter. "Blew my natural mind. And I pulled out every trick I'd ever learned and he met me stroke for stroke." Her gaze drifted off as if she were back in the bedroom.

Regina's brows rose almost to her hairline.

She blinked and returned her attention to Regina. "Needless to say, the big problem is he's still in love."

"Oh . . . sorry," she murmured for lack of something substantial to offer.

Kelly shrugged. "He still calls and we still get together." Her previous bubbly voice lost some of its bounce. "Hey, in this day and age you take what you can get."

"Do you really feel that way?"

"Sure. Don't you? Half the black men are either in jail, on drugs, or married. The other half is suspect at best. So when you find someone halfway decent you hold on to them, even if you do have to share them."

"I used to think that way."

"What changed you?"

"Finally realizing that I deserved better and that I shouldn't settle for anything or anyone that didn't make me happy."

Kelly looked her over. "Sounds easier said than done."

"Hmph, it is. I lost some things along the way, but I gained much more."

"What was that?"

"My self-respect."

Kelly gave her a crooked smile. "Well, I guess I'm not quite ready to spend the night with just me and my self-respect."

"At least you're honest. Hopefully that man of yours will see the value of that and do the right thing."

"There's always hope, and when that doesn't work, there's always G-strings!"

They laughed.

"So can I interest you in anything else?"

"I think I will take the bra and panties and the cinnamon number."

Kelly winked. "Good choice. Come on up front and I'll ring you up. Cash or charge?"

"Charge." Regina reached into her purse for her wallet, while Kelly rang up her purchases. Regina handed Kelly her credit card.

Kelly looked at the card, then at Regina. Her throat went dry. "Uh, can I see a driver's license?"

"Sure." She pulled her license out of her wallet. "Here ya go."

Kelly took the card and tried to keep her hands from shaking. She wasn't sure if it was from shock, embarrassment, anger, or all three. She pressed her lips together to force herself from saying what was on her mind. She handed back the credit card and license without a word.

Regina frowned slightly. "Something wrong?"

"No." She avoided Regina's gaze as she put her purchases in a neat little shopping bag with the store's logo of a woman's silhouette on the side. "Thanks."

"Thank you," Regina said with a hint of hesitation. "Hope everything works out for you. Um, I know this may be a strange request but . . . is there a dressing room where I can change?"

"In the back, next to the restroom."

"Thanks."

Regina picked up the shopping bag and headed to the back of the store. She shut the door behind her and got undressed and put on the cinnamon-colored outfit. She looked at her reflection in the triple mirrors. Kelly was right, it matched her skin tone perfectly. She looked as if she were totally naked except for the flowers.

She turned to get a better back view and was very pleased with the presentation and knew that

Parker would be as well. She ran her hands over the sheer clinging fabric and couldn't wait until she felt Parker's hands instead.

Regina put her street clothes back on and placed her discarded undies in the bottom of the shopping bag and returned to the front of the store.

"Perfect," Regina said, beaming.

"I know my stuff," Kelly said.

"That you do." She picked up a business card from a small holder on the counter. "And if you are as right about the response as you were about this outfit, I should have a memorable night."

Kelly's stomach tightened. "Hmmm." She forced a smile and wagged her finger. "There's always the G-string. Come by anytime."

"I'll keep that in mind." Regina smiled. "Take care." She turned and walked out.

Kelly didn't know if she should just leave well enough alone or make that call. The problem was she'd never simply left well enough alone.

Chapter 16

Parker stepped out of the shower, wrapped a towel around his waist, and hustled into the kitchen to check on dinner. He wasn't the greatest cook in the world but he'd never starve. He'd thought about ordering dinner and having it delivered, but he really wanted this to be a special night—with all the personal touches.

He opened the oven and tested the roasting chicken and baked potatoes. Another twenty minutes and everything would be done. There was a salad chilling in the fridge along with a bottle of Regina's favorite wine. He privately hoped that he could convince her to stay the night, but he didn't want to bet money on it.

Back in his bedroom, he rifled through the closet for something to put on. Regina had called on her cell phone from the road and said she'd arrive in about a half hour, which gave him around ten minutes to finish up.

Putting on a pair of jeans and a T-shirt, he slipped

his feet into his favorite loafers, went into the living room, and turned on the CD player. He took a quick look around. Everything looked cool.

He was just about to take a seat and wait when the phone rang. He hoped it wasn't Regina saying she'd be late. Crossing the room, he picked up the phone and crossed his fingers.

"Hello?"

"Uh . . . hello?"

Parker frowned slightly. "Yes, hello. Who's this?"

"It's Tracy."

The muscles in his gut tightened.

"Tracy . . . hi, sweetie."

"Mom is in the hospital and . . . I'm scared."

"What happened?"

"She got real sick and the ambulance came."

"Is there anyone with you? Where are you?"

"I came by myself with Mom. I'm in the waiting room on the pay phone."

He heard the tremors in her voice and his heart ached. Parker took a breath. "Okay, listen to me, sweetheart, is there a doctor or someone nearby?"

"No."

"What's the name of the hospital?"

"Berkley University Hospital."

"Okay. I want you to hang up but stay by the phone. I'm going to call the hospital directly and see if I can get some information. Does the pay phone have a number?"

"Yes, 713-555-8888."

He jotted down the number. "Okay, you wait right there. I'll call you back."

She sniffed. "I'm scared."

"I know, baby. But everything is going to be okay,"

he said with as much confidence as the lie would allow. Everything would be far from okay ever again. "I'll call you back."

He depressed the button and quickly redialed the hospital.

"Berkley University."

"Yes, I need some information on a patient that was just brought in by ambulance."

"Name," the woman said with as much enthusiasm as someone in a coma.

"Lynn Heywood."

He listened for what seemed like an eternity before the woman came back online.

"We have no one here by that name."

"My daughter just called from the waiting room. She said . . . Check Lynn Waverly," he said, realizing that Lynn was probably using her maiden name.

"Hold on."

The wait was interminable.

"Yes, we have a Lynn Waverly."

"Can you tell me how she is?"

"She was admitted to intensive care. That's all the information I can give you, sir."

"Thank you. Uh . . . my daughter, she's there alone. I'm in New York. Is there any way someone can sit with her?"

"You'd have to call the social work department."

"Can you transfer me?"

"Hold."

Parker paced as he listened to a series of clicks, then some music, and then the dreaded automated voice mail system advising him that no one was currently available to take his call but he was free to leave a message. He slammed down the phone, then picked it up and dialed Tracy. She picked up on the second ring.

"Dad?"

His heart knocked in his chest. It had been so long since he'd heard her say those words.

"Yeah, baby, it's me. I'm going to be on the next flight out. I want you to stay where you are. It's going to take me a while to get there. But don't leave. Do you have any money with you?"

"I have about eight dollars."

"Okay. If you get hungry ask someone where the cafeteria is. Get yourself something to eat and come straight back to the waiting room."

"Okay."

"Do you have a pen and paper?"

"Just a minute."

He heard some rustling and the phone dropping. Finally, Tracy came back on the line.

"Hello?"

"Take this number. This is my cell phone."

"Okay."

"You call if anything else happens." Then he thought about the hours in flight when he would be inaccessible. "Take this number too. It's to a friend of mine. Her name is Regina. If you get scared or need anything before you can reach me, call her, she will know what to do." He gave her the number. "I'll be there as soon as I can, Tracy. Everything will be fine. Do you have a friend you can call, a parent who can stay with you?"

"Not really. Is Mom gonna be okay?"

He hesitated, knowing the truth. "The doctors are going to do the best they can to make her feel better."

"Please hurry," she said, her voice weak and thready.

"I'm on my way, on my way. I love you, Tracy."

"Thanks."

Parker hung up the phone and dashed off to his bedroom. He pulled a suitcase out of the closet and started tossing clothes inside, just as the front doorbell rang.

Parker hurried to the front door and pulled it open to see Gina standing on the other side with a smile on her face.

"Hi, sweetheart." She leaned forward to kiss his cheek and noticed the look of distress on his face. She touched his shoulder. Her brow creased with concern. "What's wrong?"

"Come in." He started back inside, talking while he walked. "I just got a call from Tracy. Her mother has been admitted into the hospital." He proceeded on into his bedroom.

Regina immediately noticed the opened and half-packed suitcase on the bed. "Tell me what you need."

Parker's pulse slowed for the first time since he'd taken the call from his daughter. He turned to Regina, and seeing the look of concern and understanding reflected in her eyes, he knew all over again why he was in love with her. He stretched out his hand.

Regina came to him and clasped his hand in hers. They both sat down on the side of the bed.

"What happened?" she said, her voice unloosening the knots in his stomach.

"I don't know really. Can't get much information from the hospital. Tracy said her mother got really sick and went to the hospital in an ambulance. Tracy's there by herself."

"Oh no. Doesn't she have any family out there?"

"Hmph, when Lynn made her break and moved out to the coast she cut ties with everyone. Her parents are deceased and her one sister was in England the last time I heard."

"Tracy must be terrified."

"I need to get to the airport." He looked at her. "I'm really sorry about this . . . about tonight."

"Don't even worry about it. Can I help you with anything while you finish packing?"

He remembered the food in the oven and slapped the heel of his palm against his head. "Dinner."

"I'll take care of it." She left him in the bedroom and went out to the kitchen.

Parker finished packing, taking everything he thought would be necessary, not even knowing how long he would be gone. He checked his wallet for his identification and stuck it in the back pocket of his pants.

Regina poked her head inside. "I took everything out of the oven, wrapped it up, and put in the freezer so it wouldn't spoil."

He nodded. "Thanks."

"I guess you don't know how long you'll be gone."

Parker zipped the suitcase. "No, I have no idea just how serious it is with Lynn or what's—"

"Well, if you need anything, need me to check on things, make calls, whatever, just let me know as soon as you get settled."

"Thanks, babe, and thanks for understanding."

"Need a lift to the airport?"

"That would be great. Can I leave you my car keys? Then you can move my car for me. You know how it is with alternate side parking."

"I'll take care of it for you."

Parker took a breath and stood. "I guess I'd better go. I have no idea when the next flight is."

"Okay, let's go then."

"I gave Tracy your home phone number," Parker said as they sped along the Grand Central Parkway to LaGuardia Airport. "I know I should have asked first but—"

"It's not a problem. If she calls, I'll handle it."

Parker nodded and stared out of the window. "I don't know how I'm going to handle telling Tracy what's really going on. It was so unfair of Lynn to do this to her—keep her in the dark. The whole thing has been unfair from the beginning—the way she handled it, just up and left without a word."

"Don't focus on that now. The main thing is getting to Tracy and making sure that she's all right and feels safe with you."

"She doesn't even know me," he said, the pain and disgust evident in his tone. "I'm surprised she called me. But it really blew me away when she said she didn't really have any friends that she could call to sit with her or go to their house until I arrived. What kind of life are they living out there?" He slammed his fist against the side of the door, then pressed it to his chin. "Damn it. I should have found a way to be there for Tracy years ago. I should have been able to find her."

"Parker, come on, let's be real. It's not like you didn't try. This is not your fault. It's only your fault if you don't do anything about what's happening now. You can't go back and redo anything."

"In my head I know, but in my heart . . ." He shook his head. "It's a different story."

"Which line do you want to try?"

"Continental. Hopefully they'll have a flight out sometime today."

Regina wound her way around the terminal and pulled up in front of the Continental departure entrance.

"I'll circle around a couple of times, just in case you need to go to another terminal."

"If I can get a flight, I'll call you on your cell and let you know."

"Okay." She reached in her purse, took out her phone, and turned it on.

Parker leaned across the gearshift and clasped the back of her head in the palm of his hand, pulling her close. He looked into the softness of her eyes. "I love you, G. But I guess you know that by now. Things aren't going to be easy, but I'm willing to try if you are."

"We'll get through it," she said.

A security guard came up to the car and tapped on the window. "Gotta move it along. You can't park here."

Parker turned back to Regina. "I better go. I'll call you." He kissed her quickly and got out of the car.

Regina popped the trunk and Parker took out his bag. He came around to the side and leaned down to the window. "Thanks." He dug his hands into his pockets and pulled out his car keys and the keys to the house and handed them to her through the window.

She took the keys. "Go. Go. Take care of your daughter." Regina smiled and waved, slowly pulling off.

As she wound her way around the airport she
thought about Parker's impending trip and the
first meeting with his daughter in more than eight
years. She didn't envy him and wished that she could
be there. She couldn't imagine what it must be like
for Tracy, how afraid and alone she must feel. When
Parker brought her back she planned to do all that
she could to make Tracy feel welcome. She would
definitely have to get her own home in order in
the meantime.

Chapter 17

Mike Nichols sat in front of his computer, keying in information and completing all the customary searches. He'd already accumulated a pile of information on Victoria. How much of it was relevant was up for grabs.

His years with the NYPD had definitely paid off. He knew just what kind of programs to install that could track a needle in a haystack. In the ensuing years since his retirement from the force he'd mastered the art of hacking. So what he couldn't find out by traditional means, he had other ways of getting.

There was a knock on his office door.

"Come in, Leslie."

Leslie came in with a folder in her hand. "I pulled this together from what you gave me earlier." She stepped up to his desk and placed the folder on top of it, then sat down on the edge of the desk.

Mike leaned back in his squeaky chair, picked up the folder, and flipped it open. His eyes raced

over the information, taking in what was important and discarding the rest. He looked up at
Leslie.

"It appears that Mrs. Hunter is not all she claims
to be," he said.

Leslie braced her hand on her hip. "Looks that
way." Her right brow rose.

"Book me on the next flight to Atlanta. I want to
check this out myself."

"Sure." She hopped down off the desk, braced
her palms on the desk, and leaned forward, reveal-
ing a hint of abundant cleavage. "Need any company?" Her ruby-red lips curved into a provocative
smile of invitation.

Mike's eyes darkened. "Make that two tickets.
And get us a nice place to stay." He returned her
smile and reached out to stroke her hip.

Leslie grabbed his hand and placed it back down
on the cluttered desk. "I love the waiting game.
Don't you?" she teased, then turned and sauntered
out of the room, hips swaying. She tossed him a
look over her shoulder and winked.

Mike sat back and chuckled. Having your wife as
your assistant definitely had its advantages, he
mused.

He picked up the phone and called Phillip's office on Wall Street, hoping to catch him before
he'd left for the day. Phillip was emphatic about
not being contacted at home.

The phone rang until Phillip's voice mail came
on. Mike left a quick message, hung up, and called
Phillip's cell phone.

He answered on the third ring.

"Hey, Phil, it's me, Mike."

Phillip glanced in his rearview mirrors and eased

to an empty spot by the curb in front of a fire hydrant.

"Did you find anything?"

"I found something. I'm just not sure what it is yet. Let me ask you something. How much do you know about your wife's background?"

"Not a whole lot, to be truthful. She said she grew up in Chicago, that her father was deceased and her mother had remarried some land developer, but she hadn't been in touch with her in years. She's an only child."

Mike frowned. That was so far from the information he'd found that for a moment he thought he may have been investigating the wrong person.

"I see."

"What is it?"

"Let's just say that there's more to the story than that; at least it appears that way. I'm heading to Atlanta."

"Atlanta, why?"

"That's where the information is leading me. I'll keep you posted."

Phillip hesitated for a moment, not completely processing the information. "Okay," he finally said. "Do that," he added in a faraway voice.

"It's probably nothing. We get false leads all the time, but I try to check out every one."

"What's in Atlanta?"

"That's what I'm going to find out."

Kelly closed the cash register and shut off the lights. The visit earlier by Regina had upset her more than she was willing to admit. It was one thing to hear about the other woman, but to meet her in the flesh was a different story.

Regina was the kind of woman she always wanted to be: confident in her self-worth, attractive, and intelligent. Most of Kelly's life she'd spent putting on airs to get the attention she sought. She'd done everything from a nose job, to breast implants and hair weaves. All it netted her were men who wanted someone else.

But it was apparent that Regina had no real interest in rekindling her past. Kelly had every intention of getting what she wanted this time, and Regina was going to help her get it whether she realized it or not.

Charles got into his car and headed to Manhattan. He'd thought long and hard about his relationship with Toni. He still loved her and probably always would. That's what hurt the most.

From the beginning he'd done everything in his power to make her happy, giving up parts of himself in the process. Over the years he had somehow disappeared, turned into a man he didn't recognize, one who was complacent, unambitious, not the man that he'd believed himself to be. What happened with Toni and that man was as much his fault as it was hers. He'd sat back and let her drift away from him. But that didn't take away the sting of what she'd done, or excuse it. No matter how difficult things had gotten between them over the years, it never occurred to him to soothe his problems or his ego in the bed of another woman.

Some nights he would lie awake and remember

how good it had once been between them, how happy they were. And then, suddenly, they weren't and the life they'd built together came falling down around them. What was worse was that his son, Steven, was caught in the middle.

How could he ever expect his son to grow up to be a man that was honored and respected when his own father had been walked over like a welcome mat by the woman he loved? That was not the example he wanted to set for his son. But at the same time there was a part of him that wanted to hold on to that old life, find a way to forgive her and allow them to move on—together.

It was a battle that he'd fought daily. Moving out had not helped. He missed having her there beside him.

He pulled up in front of the house that Toni built—their home. He turned off the engine and stared up at the windows. After several moments he got out, set the alarm, and walked up the stone steps to the front door. He took out his key and inserted it into the lock.

It had to reach this point, he concluded as he stepped inside the familiar surroundings. He'd sat on the fence of indecision too long. Tonight that was all going to change—one way or the other.

Chapter 18

Kelly got behind the wheel of her leased midnight-blue BMW and eased out into the early evening traffic. Sitting at a red light, she watched as a couple crossed in front of her. They were holding hands, laughing, and smiling at each other. A pang of jealousy shot through her and she had the irrational urge to put her foot on the gas.

She really hated it when she began to feel this way, when the dark and lonely feelings would engulf her and she felt like hurting herself or someone else. Loneliness was a terrible thing. No one understood how crippling it could be, what it often forced her to do.

A blast from a car horn jerked her out of her musings and she sped across the intersection. It was a shame that some people had so much and others had to scrape for every little crumb. It was so unfair. She was only thirty-five years old and some days she felt like ninety. Sure, she could put on airs with the best of them, make herself look good, smell good, talk good, whatever it took to make the moments last. But it was never enough. She was never enough.

She drove down Atlantic Avenue through the heart of Ft. Greene en route to her overpriced apartment on South Oxford, when she passed the same bookstore she'd passed a million times but never paid much attention to: Regina's Place.

Kelly frowned, more annoyed by the coincidence than anything else. Could it be the same Regina? She kept driving. What were the odds of that? She turned up the volume on the radio, hoping that the light jazz would soothe her spirit.

As the sun began to set behind the rows of apartment and office buildings, the lights came on in the myriad of local lounges and cafés as the merry made their way to their favorite after-work hangout spots.

She should call Cherry, her next-door neighbor, and see if she wanted to have a drink at Royston's, but thought better of it. Cherry talked incessantly, and tonight Kelly felt like being listened to. She drove past Royston's, past her building, and out of the neighborhood. Before she realized what she was doing she was on the Brooklyn Queens Expressway, and when the reality hit her she actually smiled for the first time in hours. There was no reason why she had to keep a lid on her feelings, keep them bottled up inside and out of everyone's way. No, it was time someone listened to the real truth once and for all.

Weary from the events of the day and the letdown of the evening, Regina put her key in the door and stepped inside. All during the ride back from the airport, she worried about Parker, specifically his state of mind. She couldn't imagine what that must feel like not to have seen your child in more than eight years and then when you do it's due to such a traumatic experience. Not to mention what Tracy must be feeling. She was going to need the loving touch of a woman, and much sooner than both she and Parker anticipated. Her maternal instincts rushed to the surface and she wished she could be there for Parker and for Tracy. As much as her own mother, Millicent, got on her last nerve, she knew how much it would hurt to lose her—and she was a grown woman.

She opened the hall closet and put her purse on the top shelf, then hung up her lightweight leather jacket. The scent of spaghetti sauce floated to her nose and woke up her stomach. She smiled as she shut the closet door. Michele must really want to get back in her good graces in a hurry if she started dinner without being asked.

"I'm home," she called out as she walked toward the kitchen.

The room was empty of bodies but the pots were simmering merrily on the stove. She walked over and lifted the lids. She smiled at the wilted spaghetti and the meat sauce that was bubbling down to a paste. She lowered the flames and added some water and additional seasonings to the sauce, took the spaghetti off the stove, poured it into a strainer, and ran it under icy cold water, hoping to regain some consistency.

"Hi, Mom."

Regina turned from the sink and smiled. "Hey, Michele. Thanks for getting things started." She wanted to tell her that she needed to pay more attention to what she was doing, but thought better of it. Michele was already feeling as if she were being put upon—right or wrong. What she needed was some ego building.

"Sorry, I was doing homework."

"No problem. Where's your brother?"

"Watching television, where else?"

"Everything is just about done. You guys can eat whenever you get ready. I'm going to lie down for a while. Did anyone call?"

"No."

"Okay, thanks." She headed off to her bedroom.

No sooner had she gotten out of her work clothes and put her sexy purchases away than she heard the faint sound of the doorbell. Probably someone for the kids, she mused, and headed to the bathroom for a quick shower. That little respite was halted by a knock on her bedroom door.

"Yes!" she called out.

"Someone for you, Ma," Michele called back.

Regina frowned. "Who is it?" She rebuttoned her blouse and shut off the water.

"Kelly."

The name didn't register at all. Sighing in annoyance, she left her bedroom hoping to get rid of whoever was selling whatever as quickly as possible.

Michele was still standing guard at the front door when Regina walked up and immediately recognized the woman from the lingerie shop. At first she smiled but the smile quickly disappeared when she tried to puzzle together what she was doing there in the first place and how Kelly even knew where she lived.

"Kelly?" Regina said, frowning slightly. She stepped around Michele.

"I want to talk to you," Kelly said without preamble.

"Go on inside, Michele."

Michele gave Kelly a long look before turning and walking away.

Regina braced her hand against the door frame. "What's going on? And how did you know where I live?"

"From your credit card information and driver's license."

Regina's pulse began to pound. "Was there some problem with the card? You could have just called. I can't imagine that you pay customers personal visits," she said, annoyance tingeing her voice at the audacity of this woman.

"It's not about your card, Regina. It's about Parker."

"Parker?"

"Yes, Parker Heywood. He's your man, isn't he? Or at least you think he is."

"Look, what is this about?"

"I've been seeing Parker. I guess he never told you. I didn't put it all together until you left."

For an instant Regina was stunned speechless, but she quickly recovered.

"I don't know what kind of game you're playing, but I'm not going to indulge you. Now I'd appreciate it if you'd find your way out the same way you found yourself here."

She started to close the door, but Kelly pushed it back.

"Wait, you need to listen to me. Parker lives in

SoHo in a studio apartment. He's an artist and teaches art class at Pratt Institute."

The pulse in Regina's temple began to pound.

"He has a chocolate birthmark on his right hip," she added, reveling in the look of stunned disbelief that registered in Regina's eyes. "You can keep seeing him if you want, but we're having a baby in about six months. He may think he loves you, but he's going to be with me and our baby."

With that she turned and walked away.

Regina stood frozen in place. She wanted to run after the crazy woman and shake the lies out of her, make her take back the things she said. But she couldn't move. Finally, mechanically she closed the door. Shaken, she turned and faced her daughter, who was standing in the archway of the living room.

"Told you I didn't like him," she said, vindication lifting her voice. She turned and walked into her bedroom, shutting the door quietly behind her.

Regina felt ill.

Chapter 19

Charles pulled up in front of the house that Toni built. He glanced up at the lights in the window and thought again about what he'd come to do. The past few months had been a living hell. He was torn between the love he still felt for his wife and what her behavior had done to their marriage.

All he'd ever wanted to do was make her happy. In doing so, he'd given up a part of himself in the process. Year after year he became less and less of a participant in their marriage, reducing himself to a quiet observer. It was easier, he'd rationalized, easier than having to battle Toni for every inch of ground. He was as much at fault as she was for what had happened. He understood that. Yet, even at the lowest points in their marriage he never would have crossed the line and tried to soothe his ego or his frustration in the bed of another woman.

That was the battle he'd been fighting from the moment he found out what happened between her and Alan. Every night since then he'd struggled with the notion of forgiveness. At first he was too angry, too hurt even to think clearly. After the anger passed he experienced an odd sense of mourning, the kind of mourning you feel when someone has died.

He turned off the car, stepped out, and set the alarm. Slowly walking up the stone steps to the front door, he stuck his key in the lock and stepped into the familiar surroundings. A pang of regret echoed in his chest. They'd been happy here once upon a time, he thought, looking around. To the casual observer everything looked perfect and in its place, but no one truly knew what went on behind closed doors. The worst part of it all was what it was doing to Steven. He was going through a time in his life when he needed both of his parents. But Charles was no longer able to make that kind of personal sacrifice, even for his son. There had to be another way, and that's why he'd come.

Taking a deep breath, he walked inside, knowing from experience that he would find Toni hunched over the kitchen table reviewing her case files for the day.

When he stood at the threshold and saw her there as he'd predicted, for a moment all the ugliness disappeared. She was chewing on the end of the pencil, murmuring to herself as she was wont to do, while her eyes danced over the pages of handwritten notes. She twisted the ends of her hair between her fingers, an old habit he'd teased her about over the years.

What he saw was the one woman who'd made him smile, who warmed his soul the way no one else ever had. How could she have done this to them? How?

* * *

Toni sensed his presence and looked up, dropping the pencil to the table in the process. A look of surprise, expectation, and fear took turns dancing in her eyes.

"Charles," she whispered.

"I know I should have called first."

"It's . . . okay." She quickly gathered up her papers into a pile and nervously patted her hair and smoothed the front of her snow-white blouse. "Can I get you anything? Did you eat? I could fix—"

He held up his hand. "No. It's cool. I'm fine." He came closer. "I want to talk to you."

Toni's breathing escalated a notch. Her voice shook when she spoke. "Sure. You, uh, want to talk in here or in the living room?"

"Here is fine." He pulled out a chair and sat down.

Toni clasped and unclasped her hands, then tugged on her bottom lip with her teeth.

Charles took a breath, looked down at the table, then across and into the eyes of his wife. "This has been hard, T," he began. "I'm not really sure most days if I'm coming or going. At first I was too pissed off to even think straight. That's why I had to finally move out, to get some space and try to clear my head."

Toni swallowed hard, too afraid to speak, not sure if she wanted to hear what was coming.

"I need you to tell me why you did it. I need to understand your reasons. And please don't tell me that it just happened."

Toni glanced away. Her eyes momentarily filled. How could she explain something she didn't quite understand herself? She'd had an affair with an ex-patient. Not only was it ethically wrong, it was morally wrong as well. The worst part of it all was that the sex with Alan was what bound her. She found herself almost addicted to his lovemaking at the risk of everything. She cared for Alan in a real way. But she loved her husband, that much she was sure of. However, somewhere along the line Charles had stopped satisfying her, not simply in their day-to-day existence but in a very sexual way as well. She was starving for stimulation of her mind and her body. How could she explain that to Charles? By nature she knew herself to be one who desperately needed to "fix" people, to change them somehow. There came a point in her marriage when that challenge no longer existed and she sought her needs elsewhere.

As painful as it was to watch the anguish in his eyes, Toni began to explain what ultimately led to the downfall of their marriage.

"None of this is your fault," she concluded slowly. "I'm probably more messed up inside than I want to admit." She dared to look at him. "I never wanted to hurt you."

"But you did, in ways that you can't begin to imagine. Why didn't you just leave me, make up some excuse, and leave me?"

Her heart hammered in her chest. "Because I still love you."

"How could you love me and do this to me, to us, to Steven? From the beginning it's always been what you wanted, Toni. Don't you see that? What kind of relationship can survive when there is that kind of selfishness at the core of it?"

"I know that now. I do." She reached for his hand,

expecting him to pull away, but he didn't. Hope floated in her stomach. "I was wrong. I should have talked to you and explained then what I'm saying now."

Charles's jaw clenched. "Are you in love with him? Look me in the eye and tell me the truth."

She shook her head. "No. I'm not."

Charles heaved a sigh and pushed himself up from the table. "Let's finish talking inside." He walked into the living room and Toni followed him out.

He sat on the couch and asked her to sit beside him.

"Where's Steven?"

"He asked if he could spend the night at his friend's house."

Charles leaned back against the seat cushion and closed his eyes for a moment. "When I met you that afternoon in the bar, I just knew from the very beginning that it was going to be forever, ya know?" He opened his eyes and turned to look at her.

"Yeah, I know," she said on a breath. "I felt the same way."

He angled his body on the couch to better face her. "I know things haven't been great. . . ."

They talked for the next two hours, opening themselves up to each other in ways they'd never done in all the years of their marriage. Toni spoke candidly of her childhood, her fear of poverty and not having things. He talked about his own ambitions, his long-standing desire to own his own limo business and how he'd been putting it all into the works to surprise her, make her proud.

They talked about Steven and the problem he'd had with drugs and the police and what they could do to protect him and make him a strong man. They talked like a couple, something they should have done long ago and often.

Little by little the barricades that they'd built around each other began to come down, leaving them open and vulnerable. Talking was not only a release but an aphrodisiac as potent as any gadget in a plain brown wrapper.

Charles reached out for her and stroked her hair, heated her with his eyes. He ached for her and he could tell by the rapid rise and fall of her breasts and the wanton look in her gaze that she still wanted him, too.

He stood and pulled her up with him. He cupped her chin in his palm and lowered his head until his mouth tentatively brushed against hers.

The spark was instantaneous and sharp and Charles pulled her closer, exploring the familiar terrain of her mouth.

Toni wrapped her arms desperately around him as if afraid it was all a dream and he would vanish from in front of her.

They clung to each other, the months of loneliness and hurt dissipating by degrees.

Charles eased back, his eyes dark and demanding. "Come upstairs," he commanded, his voice raw and rough with need.

Once in the bedroom they'd shared, they were at each other like hungry teens, pulling off clothes, popping buttons, snapping hooks until they tumbled into bed, their bodies entwined.

Charles pulled Toni beneath him as she opened her legs and wrapped them tightly around his waist.

When he slowly and deliberately entered her it was as if time and space had disappeared. The months that they'd been apart fueled their passion for each other and they made love with an almost frenzied determination.

Charles whispered her name over and over like a chant as one rippling sensation after another pounded through her.

Her body shook with pleasure, almost stunned by the intensity that she felt. This was what she'd been longing for, the unbridled passion, the unrelenting need that Charles stirred in her, something that had been missing between them for far too long.

His mouth covered her right breast, taunting her nipple between his teeth, and she cried out in delight. She held his head there as she lifted her hips to meet his thrusts, knowing from experience that he was close to climax, and she wanted to be right there with him.

When it came, it was like the sun bursting over a once-dark horizon, hot and intense and utterly perfect.

As she felt him shudder deep within her, she closed her eyes and smiled. She had her husband back and she silently vowed to do everything in her power to keep him. She rested her head in the hollow of his shoulder and they slept, locked together.

Toni adjusted her body in the bed, searching in the darkness for the warmth that was oddly missing. She opened her eyes and looked to her left. The bed was empty. Slowly she sat up and rubbed her eyes, pushing her tousled hair away from her face. She listened for sounds of movement in the house and heard nothing.

"Charles."

Her call was met by silence. She leaned over and turned on the night-light. Propped up against the lamp was a white envelope. A sensation of dread filled her. With trepidation she reached for the envelope and took out the contents.

It was from the law firm of Berger and Green— divorce papers.

Chapter 20

The ride from the airport to Berkley University Hospital seemed to take almost as long as the five-and-a-half-hour flight from New York. Parker was certain he could run faster than the cab was driving.

"Isn't there another route you could take?" he shouted through the Plexiglas partition.

The driver looked at him through the rearview mirror. "Not if you want to get there tonight. Traffic is bad all over."

"How much longer?" Parker asked as they came to another grinding halt.

The driver shrugged. "At this pace about another twenty minutes."

Parker checked his watch. It was nine-fifteen West Coast time. Tracy had been alone for hours. He felt like jumping out of his skin. Finally resigning himself to the fact that barking at the driver wasn't going to get him to the hospital any faster, he sat back and tried to imagine what he would say to

Tracy when he saw her and how she would react when she saw him.

She was six years old when Lynn disappeared with her. It had been nearly nine years since he'd set eyes on his daughter. He wondered how much she'd changed. Did she still look like her mother or had any of his genes finally kicked in?

To this day he could never wrap his mind around how Lynn could have been so cruel as to take Tracy away from him. He adored his daughter and doted on her like the little princess she was.

Did she remember the times they shared playing in the park, or the trip to Disney World, or their talks at night about the great artist she would be when she grew up? Did she remember the visits to the museums and art galleries or the hours he spent teaching her how to mix colors?

He did. He remembered every minute. For eight years those memories were all that he'd had to hold on to.

"Thirty-five dollars," the driver announced, pulling into the winding driveway of the hospital.

Parker looked up to find himself on the hospital grounds. He reached inside his jacket and pulled out his wallet, took out two twenties, and handed them to the driver. "Keep the change," he mumbled. He got out of the cab and pulled his suitcase off the seat. "Thanks." He shut the door and walked to the entrance, his steps slower than he'd anticipated as the veracity of what was about to happen was only moments away.

He went straight to the information desk and was directed to the third floor. He stepped off the elevator, looked for signs to the nurses' station, and started down the hushed corridor. The sight of a glass-enclosed room halted him in his tracks.

There she was. His heart began to race and his stomach tightened. He stepped closer to get a better look at his sleeping beauty before she awoke and noticed him. She still had the same oval face, tawny complexion, and honey-blond hair. She had a light dusting of freckles across her nose that he didn't remember, but everything else was the same, right down to the identical birthmark that they shared, hers on her wrist and his on his hip. He always used to tease her that it was the only thing chocolate about her. And she would giggle, flashing matching dimples, and say that she was all chocolate on the inside where it really counted.

He entered the room, approaching quietly, and sat down beside her. Gently he brushed aside her hair from her face and she stirred in her sleep.

"Tracy," he said softly so as not to startle her.

Her eyes fluttered open, a momentary look of confusion registered in her gaze. She sat up and eased away to get a better look.

"Daddy?"

Parker nodded. "Yes, baby, it's me." A lump formed in his throat. He wanted to hold her close but dared not.

Her eyes filled with tears and spilled over her cheeks. She pressed her head against his chest and held him, crying his name over and over.

Parker held her tight, wanting to squeeze away her pain even as he tried to soothe her with comforting words of assurance.

By degrees, her crying slowly subsided and she

sniffed back the remnants of her tears and wiped her eyes with the back of her hand.

"I didn't think you would come," she said, her voice wobbling like a baby learning to walk.

He caressed her cheek. "I told you I would be here."

"Have you seen Mom?"

"No. Not yet." He looked around. "Let me check in with the nurse and let them know I'm here." He got up and she frantically grabbed his hand. "It's okay, sweetie. I'll be right back. I need to find out where your mother is and how she's doing, okay?"

Numbly she nodded and reluctantly released his hand.

Parker tugged in a breath, gave her a tight smile, and walked out. In the hallway, he could hear the faint sounds of moaning, the sound of people in pain. He pushed the sounds out of his head and approached the nurses' station.

"Excuse me. I'm Parker Heywood. My wife . . . ex-wife was brought in earlier today."

The middle-aged nurse looked up and smiled benignly at him. "What's the patient's name?"

"Lynn Waverly."

She turned to a computer screen and typed in some information. When she looked up at him he could sense that she was forcing herself to remain cheery.

"She's in room 787. But you'll need to put on a sterile gown, mask, and gloves before you go in."

Parker frowned. "Why?"

The nurse swallowed hard. "Do you know why Ms. Waverly was brought in?"

"No. I received a call from my daughter saying

that her mother got sick and was brought in by ambulance."

The nurse stood. "Let me see if I can find the doctor. He'll explain everything."

"What's going on?" His mind began to paint a grim picture.

"The doctor will explain."

She got up from behind the desk and walked quickly down the hall, her rubber-soled shoes making a slight squishing sound as she walked.

Parker turned toward the waiting room and saw Tracy watching the exchange. He forced a smile and mouthed that everything was okay. When he turned back, the nurse and a doctor were approaching.

"Mr. Heywood, I'm Dr. Grant." He extended his hand, which Parker shook.

"What's going on? What's wrong with Lynn?"

The doctor pursed his lips and folded his hands in front of him. "Your wife is in the final stages of AIDS. She has pneumonia in both lungs and her kidneys are failing. She was delirious when she was brought in, which is typical when the virus attacks the brain. Dementia has already set in. We've tried to make her as comfortable as possible, Mr. Heywood, but I don't think your wife will be going back home."

Parker felt the room shift and he reflexively reached for the desk to steady himself. The doctor grabbed his arm.

"Are you all right?" He turned to the nurse. "Get some water," he instructed. "Why don't we sit down over here?" He led Parker to a plastic bench against the wall.

"How long?" Parker was finally able to utter.

"Could be days or weeks, not much longer, I'm afraid."

Numbly Parker nodded. He turned to the doctor. "Do you know how long she's had it?"

"She only started coming for treatment about six months ago. Unfortunately, by that time it was really too late."

Parker was speechless. He felt as if he'd been sucker punched in the gut. He'd thought cancer for sure. It was what he'd been led to believe, or was it what he wanted to believe? He'd never gotten a straight answer from Lynn and now he knew why.

"I need to ask you this, Mr. Heywood," the doctor said. "I understand you are divorced."

"Yes."

"How long ago?"

"What?"

"How long ago were you intimate with your wife?"

"We . . . haven't been together in nearly nine years."

"I suggest you get yourself tested, Mr. Heywood. HIV can live dormant in the body for years. It's obvious from your wife's deteriorated condition that she's had it for a very long time. Somehow she's managed to live with it."

"Are you saying that I could have the virus?"

"It's quite possible. But rather than speculate, you need to be tested."

All the air seemed to stop moving in and out of his lungs and instead formed a hard knot in the center of his chest. HIV? It couldn't be possible. After they'd had Tracy, they were always careful.

Lynn didn't want any more kids. Sure, they'd taken some chances in between, but for the most part he used protection. When? How? And then it hit him.

Lynn left him for some cop, a cop named Paul. The affair had gone on for months before she finally broke down and told him.

Bile rose to his throat. *Regina.*

Chapter 21

Regina wasn't sure how long she'd sat at the kitchen table staring at the clock on the wall. She felt like doing an Angela Bassett and going over to Parker's place and setting the joint on fire. But of course she had to be rational, clearheaded Regina.

There was always the possibility that Kelly was just a deranged woman who had some unreasonable gripe against her and was making the whole thing up. And that notion was just as silly as her idea to set Parker's loft on fire. Unless Kelly moonlighted as a doctor, there was no way for her to know about his birthmark.

How could he have done this to her, to them? He swore he loved her and wanted to make a life with her and the kids. And all the while he was having a relationship with someone else. A baby. That devastated her more than anything. A fling, a short-term affair, they might have been able to weather through, but a baby . . .

"Ma, telephone."

In a daze, Regina turned to her son. "Who is it, Darren?"

"It's Dad."

She really didn't feel like talking to Russell, not tonight. "Tell him I'll call him tomorrow."

Darren looked at her. "Are you okay, Ma?"

Regina forced herself to smile. "Yes, I'm fine. Just a little tired, that's all. Tell your dad what I said, okay?"

Darren nodded and walked out of the kitchen.

Regina pushed herself up from her seat and somehow found her way to her bedroom. All she wanted to do was crawl under her covers and sleep until it all felt better.

The sound of her name stirred her from a disturbing dream. In it Victoria and Toni were sitting in the Shark Bar where they used to have their weekly get-togethers. They were taking turns at the microphone telling her and the audience what a fool she'd been to trust her heart to Parker.

"I told you that you should have stayed with Russell," Victoria scolded. Her growing belly bobbed up and down in concert with her wagging finger. "Now look at what's happened."

Toni stepped up onstage and snatched the microphone from Victoria. "I may have a lousy marriage myself, but yours was no worse than mine. You need to work on getting Russell back like I'm trying to get Charles back. You need to think of your kids, girl."

The audience was chanting wildly, "Russell, Russell, Russell!"

Russell stood in the back of the restaurant and

slowly began to walk toward her. He had a huge bouquet of flowers in his hands. Parker was at the door, shouting her name, but security wouldn't let him in.

"Regina."

Regina tried to force her eyes to stay closed. She just wanted to sleep. Even the nightmare was better than having to deal with her real life. She felt the side of the bed sink down and the presence of someone next to her.

"Gina."

A heavy hand gently touched her shoulder.

Reluctantly she opened her eyes. "Russell?"

"Hey." He smiled. "Michele said you weren't feeling well.

Regina propped herself up on her elbow. "I'm not sick, just tired, that's all." She looked away.

"I was married to you for fourteen years, Regina. I know you, remember?"

"I'm all right, Russell, and I'd really appreciate it if you left my bedroom," she said without much conviction.

"Something happen at work?"

"No," she mumbled.

"Michele isn't acting up again, is she?"

"Not in the past few hours." She laughed without humor.

"Then what is it, Gina? I've known you to stay up until the sun rose. I can't remember a time when you took to bed before midnight."

She felt her throat tighten and her eyes begin to burn. "I really don't want to talk about it."

"How about going for a drive?"

"What?"

"A drive, maybe out to the beach."

"Russell, I—"

"Indulge me. Just this once." He extended his hand.

Regina hesitated, then put her hand in his and sat up. "Let me at least wash my face."

"I'll wait for you up front."

Russell pulled into Jacob Riis Park and drove along the interior road until he reached the boardwalk. He turned off the car. "Want to walk?"

"Okay."

Russell got out and came around to open Regina's door. She stepped out into the balmy spring air. The last time she was here was nearly three years ago, the night she made her decision to leave Russell.

They walked in silence for a few moments. It was Russell who broke it.

"Gina, you don't have to say anything, I'm not expecting any answers. But please listen to what I have to say."

"All right."

"I know that our marriage was not all that it should have been. I came from the old school of thought that the only role a man had to play was one of provider, nothing more. And I tried to do that to the best of my ability, mindless of anything else." He inhaled deeply. "Over the years it got easier to have things my way. I felt it was owed to me 'cause I was taking care of business." He turned and glanced at her stoic profile. "I didn't take your needs or wants into consideration. I didn't feel I had to. I was wrong. Dead wrong.

"Since you left and struck out on your own, getting the bookstore, running it successfully, taking care of the kids, it pissed me off. I thought, who does she think she is? Does she really think she can make it without me? The thing is, you can and you have. I know I've been a real ass, trying to bum-rush my way back into your life, threatening to take the kids from you, showing up at your place unannounced." He stopped walking and turned to her. "That's not how I want things to be between us, Gina. You're an incredible woman and it took losing you for me to finally realize that. I know you probably think I'm just talking to hear myself speak, but I'm telling you the truth. There's not a day that goes by that I don't think about how I messed up a good thing and lost the only woman in my life that ever mattered."

He lowered his gaze, focusing on the sand be-neath his feet. "I . . . miss you, G. More than you can imagine. And I'm still very much in love with you. I've tried to put you out of my mind, put the kids out of my mind, just so that I could get through the day." He clasped her shoulders and looked into her startled eyes. "I still love you, maybe more now than I did before. I want to be a part of your life, a permanent part of your life. There hasn't been any-one before you or since that has made me feel the way you do, that has made me want to be a better man. And I can be, Gina. I can be the man you need if you give me a chance."

Regina was so dumbfounded she didn't know what to say. Why was he telling her all this now, now when she felt so weak and vulnerable, when her heart was aching and her emotions were torn?

"Russell—"

"Shhh." He put his index finger to her lips. "You don't have to say anything." He emitted a nervous chuckle. "Kinda scared of what you might say right now anyway."

His eyes roamed erotically over her face and she acutely remembered the way his look could spark the fires within her even when her mind rebelled against it.

Russell's hands moved from her shoulders and slid down her spine, easing her a step closer to him.

"I want to kiss you. Tell me no and I won't."

She hesitated for a fraction of a heartbeat, but that was all the encouragement he needed.

Russell lowered his head and tentatively pressed his full lips against hers. Regina felt a momentary shiver as the familiarity of his mouth rekindled the past to merge with the present. For a moment she allowed herself the full experience of it, wanting to escape her current heartache to a place where she understood the rules and the players. But this wasn't the way, she realized, as the haze of a building desire began to boil in her veins. She felt Russell's growing need for her, and had it been any other time she would have given in as she'd always done. But she wasn't that Regina anymore. She would not let her body's wanton needs overrule her mind.

She pulled away and turned her back to him, quickly pulling herself together. Russell stepped around and stood in front of her.

He lifted her lowered chin with the tip of his fingers. "I won't apologize for that, because I'm not sorry it happened," he said in a soft voice. "I want you back. It's that simple. And I'm coming for you in every way I know how and I won't stop until you tell me to."

Her stomach was spinning and her heart was beating totally out of control. Somewhere along the line she'd missed reading a chapter of the book. Who was this new man in front of her and where had her ex-husband gone?

He took her hand. "Come on, let me get you back home before I really cross the line."

"Darren! Get the phone. I'm in the bathroom," Michele shouted. "If it's Chris, tell him I'll call him right back."

Darren grumbled over the fact that he had to put his video game on pause. He went into the living room and picked up the phone.

"Hello?"

"Darren, hi, this is Parker."

"Hi."

"Is your mom there?"

"No."

Parker frowned. It was nearly midnight in New York. "Do you know where she is?"

"She went out with my dad."

Parker tried to keep his voice calm and even. "Oh. Uh, do you know how long she's been gone . . . when she'll be back?"

"Not really. She's been gone a couple of hours."

"I see. Well, when she gets in, please tell her that I called and ask her to call me on my cell phone."

"Okay," he replied absently, already thinking about his next move on the video game.

"Thanks." Parker hung up.

"Who was on the phone?" Michele asked.

Darren shrugged. "Nobody." His gaze was fixed

on the television screen as the 3-D figures raced, jumped, and pillaged at his command.

Michele shook her head and returned to her room.

Parker slowly walked back to the waiting area to get Tracy and take her home. Lynn was sedated and resting as comfortably as possible under the circumstances. He'd taken the doctor's card and promised to call the hospital in the morning to make an appointment to get tested.

If the worst-case scenario were to become real, how was he ever going to tell Regina?

As he walked to the front of the hospital with his arm around his daughter's shoulder, another question plagued him as well. What was Regina doing out with her ex-husband barely hours after she'd left him?

Chapter 22

Mike Nichols and his wife, Leslie, sat in the outer offices of the hall of records. He pulled out his notebook from his inside jacket pocket.

"I just don't get it," Mike mused. "Some folks will go to any length to get away from who they are."

"Maybe she has a good reason," Leslie offered.

"I suppose. And in this line of work I've pretty much seen it all."

"Mr. Nichols?"

"Yes." Mike stood up and walked over to the receptionist.

"Ms. Gray will see you now. You can go right in."

"Thanks." He turned to his wife. "I'll be right back." He walked into the office behind the front desk.

Ms. Gray rose when he came in. "Please have a seat, Mr. Nichols. What can I do for you?"

He pulled out his identification and placed it on the desk. "I've been retained by Mr. Phillip Hunter to track down his wife's family."

"Yes. And how can I help you?"

"After doing some investigating I found out that what my client's wife has been telling him all along hasn't been exactly true."

"I'm sure she has her reasons." She leaned back in her seat.

Mike chuckled. "Same thing my wife said." His expression grew serious. "But I need to know what those reasons are. I need to find out who she really is. And my information led me here. I know that she did grow up here, but her mother is not who she says she is. The name on the original birth certificate says Ellen Lawry is her natural mother. But the certificate that my client's wife has says that Maureen Flowers is her mother. I'd like to find this Ellen Lawry if she's still around. There should be some record of her somewhere."

"I can take you to our filing room. You're free to go through whatever public records you find. But that's all I can do."

"Fair enough."

Ms. Gray pushed back from her seat and stood. "My secretary can show you where to go."

"Thank you."

Ms. Gray watched him leave, and the moment he was out of sight she got on the phone.

Mike and Leslie pored over the records for a solid hour before Mike found what he was looking for. He jotted down some notes on his pad.

"I think this is it, babe."

Leslie leaned over. "What did you find?"

"Last-known address, family information." He shook his head. "Can't wait until I get to the bottom of this story." He stacked up the books he'd been using. "Come on, we're going to pay Ms. Lawry a visit."

Ellen hung up the phone and slowly lowered herself into the seat next to the desk. She knew this day would eventually come. She'd prayed for it and dreaded it at the same time. All these years, she thought, wasted years. There wasn't a day that went by that she didn't wonder what happened to her daughter.

"Grandma, Grandma, don't I look pretty?"

Ellen turned smiling eyes on her granddaughter, Victoria. "You look beautiful, princess. Where's Mommy?" She reached over and adjusted the collar on her dress.

"She's coming. We're going to the movies. Granddaddy says he's coming too. You wanna come, Grandma?"

"No, sweetie, not today. Maybe another time."

"Stop worrying Grandma to death," Felicia said, stepping into the room. "We should be back in a couple of hours, if she doesn't run me ragged in the meantime."

Felicia smiled and Ellen was as stunned as always by the resemblance she had to the older sister she never met. Ellen always imagined that Victoria would look exactly like Felicia when she grew up.

Felicia leaned down and kissed her mother's cheek. "See you later. Tell Dad we'll be in the car."

Moments later Ellen's husband, Will, emerged from the kitchen, and just like more than forty years ago her heart still raced at the sight of him.

"How'd I get hooked into going to see a Disney movie about a fish?" he grumbled.

Ellen laughed. "Because you'll do anything your granddaughter asks you to do."

Will chuckled. "Shame. That little vixen has me wrapped around her finger. By any chance, did they leave without me?"

"They're waiting for you in the car."

"Wish me luck. I just hope I don't fall asleep. You know how Vikki always wants to quiz me afterward about every detail of the movie." He kissed her on the lips. "Still as lovely as ever," he whispered.

"You always know what to say to a girl," she murmured, her heart filled with love. "Have a good time. Dinner will be ready when you get back."

He took his hat from the rack by the door. "See ya."

Ellen peeked through the curtains and watched them pull off. No sooner had they disappeared down the street than a dark sedan slowed to a stop in front of her house. Ellen took a deep breath, walked to the front door, and opened it.

Chapter 23

Toni decided to call in sick. There was no way that she could sit in front of her clients today and pretend that she had the answers to cure their ills. Her life was a mess. She was a mess.

She sat at the kitchen table with the same cup of coffee that had been there for the past hour. She lifted the divorce papers from the table and looked at them again. The blank space that awaited her signature seemed to scream at her, *Sign, sign*. She tossed them aside as if they'd scorched her fingers.

Toni felt like a two-dollar whore. She'd given up her body in the naive hope that she could win the brass ring. What she was going through now was indicative of her life. She'd always wanted more and more and she knew it stemmed from her deprivations as a child in Louisiana. She'd been running from her past all her life trying to fill it with things. This was the result. She'd always preached honesty to her clients, trying to impress upon them to be honest with themselves and understand the real motives for their actions. Hmph, what kind of example was she? And by the time she realized that she needed to be honest with herself and her husband it was too late.

She had to grudgingly admit that she really didn't believe that Charles had it in him to go this far. In the back of her mind, she'd convinced herself that he'd come back. He did, but not the way he wanted. She sighed heavily. What was she going to do now? Funny, her life's work was dealing with the statistics of society and now she'd become one herself.

This must be the way Charles felt, she realized as she poured the cold cup of coffee down the drain—used and betrayed. She supposed she deserved it and she had no one to blame but herself.

Aimlessly she walked around her house, looking at all the beautiful possessions. Her footsteps echoed in the emptiness. She had everything and nothing at all.

Regina couldn't seem to keep her mind on what she was doing. The information on the inventory sheet seemed to blend together into a big blur. She couldn't shake Russell's kiss out of her head or the things he'd said to her. She knew better than to be tempted by Russell's silver tongue. After all, that was how he made his living—convincing people that what he offered was just what they needed.

But that wasn't what was really bothering her and she knew it. Guilt was what kept her awake most of the night. She felt as if she'd betrayed Parker by kissing Russell, even knowing what he'd done with Kelly. She cringed. That was still a hard pill to swallow. She was confused and angry and she'd done something stupid as a result. What she needed to do was talk to Parker face-to-face and get to the bottom of things before she started jumping to conclusions and even considering jumping in bed with her ex.

"Ms. Everette, telephone," Renee called out from the front of the store.

Regina breathed a sigh of relief, thankful for the reprieve.

"Be right there," she called out. She closed the log and hopped down from the stool at her work-table. The entire setup—the leather and chrome stool, the drafting table, the gooseneck lamp—had been a present from her mother when her store celebrated its first thirty days of business. Regina had protested that the gift was much too extrava-gant, but Millicent Prescott was not to be deterred. She insisted that it was just a small token to show how proud she was of Regina and to apologize for not believing in her dream.

Regina smiled at the memory as she walked to the front of the store, stretching her spine along the way. She and her mother had certainly had their share of mother/daughter conflict, but once her mother fi-nally accepted the fact that she could not dictate Regina's life any longer, she finally backed off.

Now, after nearly forty years of living Regina's life for her, Millie had finally found a life of her own. At this very minute, her once-upon-a-time strait-laced mother was having a ball in Hawaii, with Mr. Lincoln from her church no less. Regina couldn't wait to get the details of that trip.

"Thanks, Renee," she said, picking up the phone from the front desk. One of these days she was going to have another phone installed in the back.

"Hello?"

All she heard was what sounded like labored breathing.

"Hello?"

"G . . ."

Regina frowned. She turned to Renee. "Did they say who this was?"

"No. Just asked for you. I could barely understand her."

"Hello? Who is this?"

"T . . . Toni."

"Toni! Toni, what's wrong, girl?"

"Took . . . something . . ."

"Oh, damn. Where are you?" She whirled toward Renee. "Call 911 on your cell, now! Toni, where are you?"

"Home . . . alone." She started sobbing.

"I got 911."

"Tell them to get to 101 West 127th Street and Riverside."

"Toni, what did you take?"

"Stuff . . . Lonely, G. I really screwed up this time . . ." She wept and laughed simultaneously.

"Listen to me, you don't do anything else until I get there. I sent for an ambulance. They're on the way and so am I. You stay on the phone with Renee until help comes." She snatched a look at Renee. "You keep her talking." She grabbed her purse from beneath the counter.

"About what?" Renee asked, suddenly realizing the enormity of her responsibility.

"I don't give a damn what you talk about. Recite the phone book. Just keep her talking."

Regina ran out the door. Her hands were shaking so badly that she couldn't get the key into the ignition of the car. Finally, she got it started and raced off, praying all the way on the ride across the Brooklyn Bridge, the FDR Drive, and then across town in Manhattan. The higher power was definitely with her. She made it uptown in less than an hour.

By the time she arrived at Toni's brownstone, the ambulance was gone, of course, but Toni's neighbors were still outside. Regina jumped out of her car and darted off toward an older woman who looked like she kept her eye on everyone and everything.

"Hi," Regina said a bit breathless. "I'm a friend of Antoinette Devon. I was the one who called the ambulance. Do you know what hospital they took her to?"

The woman looked her up and down. "I've seen you before."

"Yes, I'm Toni's friend Regina."

"Right. Well, they took that poor child to St. Luke. Had to kick the door down to get in." She shook her head sadly. "She hasn't been the same since her husband left. But I saw him come by last night. His car was parked out front most of the evening. I finally got tired of looking and went to bed."

Regina put the pieces of what the woman was saying together, and she didn't like the image that emerged.

"Thank you," she said, cutting her off. "I think I should get to the hospital." She went toward her car.

"Tell her Ms. Jean is praying for her," the woman called out.

"I will."

Regina pulled off, cutting across the eight blocks to the hospital in five minutes flat. She went straight to the emergency room, identified herself, and was directed to a curtained area where Toni was being treated by a nurse.

"How is she?" Regina whispered.

The nurse turned from hanging an IV bag. "She'll be fine. We had to pump her stomach. She's stable. We'll be transferring her upstairs for observation."

"Observation?"

"Yes. It's standard procedure. Any attempted suicides must be held for a minimum of forty-eight hours on the psychiatric ward."

Regina's heart seemed to stop beating for a moment. "Is she awake?"

"She's drowsy. She was given a mild sedative to help her relax." She checked the heart monitor and the speed of the IV drip. "I'll be back shortly to take her upstairs."

Regina drew in a breath and slowly approached her friend, who suddenly looked so small and vulnerable. Gone was the fiery, fast-talking, hip-switching woman. In her place was someone who looked fragile enough to break, and it seemed that she had done just that. Regina moved the wooden chair closer to the bed and reached out to gently touch Antoinette's hand.

"Hey, girl," she said softly. "It's me, Gina."

Antoinette moaned slightly and turned her head in the direction of the familiar voice. When her eyes fluttered open and settled on Regina's face, they quickly filled with tears.

"So stupid," she croaked.

"Yeah, it was," Regina teased. She reached over and brushed away Antoinette's tears. "I'm just glad you called."

"Didn't have anyone else," she said, her voice hoarse and raspy. "You're my friend."

"Always."

"He's gone for good, G."

"Who?"

"Charles."

Regina pressed her lips together, not wanting to spew out a clichéd response about how it was "going to be okay."

"Don't worry about it now. You rest and we can talk about it later."

"He's divorcing me. Left me the papers after he screwed me."

"Toni . . . I'm so sorry."

Tears rolled down Toni's cheeks. "Me too."

Regina held her hand while Antoinette haltingly told her what happened, right up to when she decided to take the sleeping pills.

"I know you may not want to hear this now, but nothing is worth taking your life over. You have a son to think about. What would Steven do without you, sweetie?"

"I know." She sniffed. "I know."

"Besides, who would I tell my troubles to?"

"There's always Vikki."

They both laughed and Regina silently prayed that she'd never be faced with the kind of decision Toni made.

Chapter 24

By the time the cab pulled up in front of Lynn's pink and white stucco house, Tracy was fast asleep. They'd spent most of the night and part of the morning at the hospital standing vigil until the doctor insisted that they both go home and get some rest. Parker paid the driver and gently shook Tracy awake.

"You're home, baby."

Groggy, she sat up and rubbed her eyes.

"Do you have your keys?"

She nodded and yawned.

"Okay, come on."

When Parker stepped inside the three-bedroom split-level home, he was not surprised by the flair with which the space was laid out. Lynn was a closet interior designer and would spend hours and great sums of money getting things to look the way she wanted them to. Even as ill as she'd become, her home was still immaculate.

"I can show you the guest room," Tracy offered.

"Thanks." He followed her down a wide hallway

that was lined with artwork, some of which he recognized as his own. A soft pang of regret knocked in his chest. They had so much potential together, he thought in a wistful moment.

They turned left down the hallway.

"Mom keeps clean towels and stuff in each bathroom."

Parker nodded and suddenly took Tracy in his arms and held her. He felt her body shudder as she fought not to cry.

"It's okay," he whispered.

"She's gonna die, isn't she? Just like Paul."

Parker's gut tightened. "Paul?"

She sniffed. "Yes. He was Mommy's friend. He got real sick. They said he had pneumonia. Same thing as Mom." She stepped back and looked up into his eyes. "I know what it is. But no one will tell me the truth." Her bottom lip trembled.

Parker swallowed hard. "Let's sit down and talk for a minute." He put his arm around her shoulder and they walked back out into the living room.

As he took a seat beside his daughter, he tried to formulate in his mind the words that could possibly explain this tragedy. How did you tell a young girl that she was on the verge of losing her mother and that she was going to have to live with a father that she didn't know?

Parker began tentatively, gauging her reactions as he spoke. For the most part she was stoic, other than the occasional tear that would escape, and she'd quickly wipe it away.

"The doctors don't know how much time she has. But I'm going to stay here until . . ." He halted and regrouped. "Then we'll make arrangements for you to come back and live with me in New York."

"What if I don't want to go?"

"What do you mean?" It never occurred to him that she would not want to come to New York. "You can't live here alone, Tracy."

"Why can't you move out here? Why do I have to leave?"

"Well . . ." He stumbled for a moment. "It's where I live. My job is there, my studio." *Regina.* "There are great schools in New York. And you'll make new friends. And I have a friend, her name is Regina. She has two kids, a girl and a boy—"

She sprang up from the seat. "I'm not going! I don't want to meet your *friend* and her kids. Put me in a home." She turned pain-filled, confused eyes on him. "I hate you!" She ran out of the room.

Moments later Parker heard Tracy's bedroom door slam in the distance. When his head cleared from the shock of what had happened, his first reaction was to go after her and demand an apology, make her listen to reason. But before he reacted to the concept he thought better of it. More pressure was not what Tracy needed. But what she did need he couldn't provide: a healthy mother who'd be there to show her what it was like to be a woman, a life that wasn't filled with lies, a life where people she cared about didn't leave her, and a father whom she both knew and loved.

She had every right to be angry. Life had played a nasty trick on her. But he must find a way to reach her and get her to believe that he was there for her and that they'd get through it together.

He sat down on the couch and covered his face

with his hands, trying to get his thoughts together. It was so much to digest. So many changes were going to have to be made, decisions and lifestyle adjustments. For both of them. The sad thing was he had no idea how to raise a teenage girl. It was pretty obvious from what had transpired that he didn't have all the answers and that he was going to need help finding them. And what of his own health? What if . . .

Suddenly exhausted, he pushed up from the couch and walked down the hallway to the guest room. He noticed a light beneath Tracy's door. He started to knock, but halted midway.

He needed to talk to Regina.

Chapter 25

Regina kept checking the phone, thinking that it must not be working. What other reason could there be for Parker not to have called her? Maybe it was best that he didn't, she mused, her ire rising once again. She didn't really think she was in the frame of mind to talk to him.

Every time she thought about him and Kelly she wanted to die inside. Was this how Charles felt when he found out about Toni and Alan? At least Toni didn't pop up pregnant on top of everything else. But what she'd wound up doing to herself was bad enough.

She picked up the phone and dialed Victoria's number. Victoria did need to know. Maybe they could both go visit Toni at the hospital later on.

The phone rang and rang until the answering machine came on. Regina left a vague message with no hint as to what happened. That wasn't the kind of information you left on someone's answering machine, she thought, and hung up the phone.

Aimlessly she moved around the kitchen rewashing dishes and wiping down clean counters. The store didn't open on Saturday until noon. She still had a couple of hours, but the last thing she felt like doing was going in to the store. She didn't think she had it in her today to put a smile on her face and pretend to be interested in her customers' wants or needs.

A wave of melancholy swept through her and she suddenly felt so weak. Everything seemed to be coming apart at the seams; her daughter was on a self-destruction mission, her ex-husband was making moves on her and messing with her head, one of her best friends tried to kill herself, and for good measure the man she was in love with was having a baby with another woman. And for the first time in a long while she felt helpless to do anything about anything. Damn it, what else could happen?

She tossed the dishrag into the sink, dried her hands on a towel, and started for her bedroom. Maybe a good hour workout at the gym would unfurl some of the tension in her body. Her neck was so stiff she felt as if it would snap in half.

In her bedroom she went to the closet and pulled out her gym bag, then filled it with her customary sweats, a clean towel, deodorant, lotion, and a change of underwear. She zipped the bag up and was ready to head out when the phone rang.

It'd better not be another trauma.

When she picked up the phone she saw that it was a number she didn't recognize.

"Hello?"

"Gina, it's me, Parker."

"Hello, Parker," she said, her voice tight and cool.

"Listen, baby, I'm sorry I didn't get to call you last night. We just came home from the hospital."

Regina took the phone and moved to the kitchen chair and sat down.

"How is she?" she forced herself to ask. She folded her arms beneath her breasts and rocked her crossed legs.

"It's not good. The doctors don't know how much longer she has. Tracy is a mess . . . I . . . don't know what do to, babe."

His voice cracked and Regina felt his pain.

"I'm sorry, Parker," she said and meant it. As much as she wanted to blast him out, call him every name but a child of God for what he'd done, she knew this wasn't the time.

"Gina . . . I need to tell you something. Please promise me that you won't freak out, that you'll listen."

Her grip tightened on the phone. "What is it?"

"It's about Lynn . . . the reason why she's . . . sick."

The pulse in her temples began to pound. "What are you trying to tell me?"

"She's dying of AIDS, Gina."

Regina felt the room shift. For an instant she couldn't breathe. She forced herself to think, calculate, figure it out. In her mind she envisioned all the times she and Parker made love, the times with protection and the times they took stupid chances. The contents of her stomach rose.

"Gina."

"Yes." The single word was almost a whimper.

"The doctor said I need to be tested. You need to be tested too, Gina. Just to be sure," he quickly added. "I'm sure that—"

"Sure! What the fuck can you be sure about,

Parker?" She was shaking all over. "Sure about what—sure about what—that you didn't contract a disease from your wife that could kill us both? Is that what you're sure about?"

"Gina. The doctor said—"

"I don't give a damn what the doctor said. HIV can live in your body for years, the years you were with her. How do I know *you* didn't give it to her?" Rage and terror roared through her like a forest fire gone out of control.

"I didn't, Gina. I didn't. I swear to you I didn't."

"Really? Can you swear to me that you didn't sleep with *Kelly* while we were together? Can you?"

"Kelly? It's not what you think."

"Go to hell, Parker." She slammed the phone down so hard in the cradle she pulled it out of the wall.

Regina stood there staring down at the plastic pieces, shaking like a leaf. She pushed her fist to her mouth to keep from screaming. *Oh God, oh God.*

Parker sat on the side of the bed, numb. He needed to get home, back to Regina. He needed to be there face-to-face. If she could only look in his eyes, she would know that he would never do anything to hurt her and that he was just as ragged inside as she was.

But he couldn't go to her. His daughter and Lynn needed him here. He felt as if his life were spinning out of control and he had no way to stop it. He wouldn't lose Regina. He couldn't. She was his world. She had to know that. But now.

Kelly. What in the world did she say to Regina?

He pounded his fist against the dresser, rattling the lamp and knocking it to the floor.

He wasn't going to let outside forces destroy everything he'd worked for. Whatever he had to do to make it right he would. One obstacle at a time.

The phone rang and he snatched it up.

"Gina!"

"Mr. Heywood, this is Dr. Grant. We need you to come to the hospital right away. Your wife is awake and asking for you."

"I'll be right there."

"I think you should bring your daughter."

Parker stood next to Lynn's bed garbed in a sterile gown. Her labored breathing vibrated in the room.

"Thank you for coming," Lynn said in a halting voice.

Gone was the raving beauty that stole his heart so many years ago. She barely weighed one hundred pounds and her veins could be seen through her nearly transparent skin that was now pale as a piece of parchment.

"You knew I would," he said gently.

"Take care of Tracy."

"I will. I promise."

"I'm so sorry . . . for everything. I never should have taken her away."

"Don't worry about that now."

"I've been sick . . . for a long time. Was afraid to tell you."

He held back his reprimand, knowing it was pointless.

"I got it from . . . Paul." Her mouth twisted into a crooked smile. "I thought I was leaving you for something better. Ironic, huh?"

"I don't know what to say, Lynn. You wanted to be happy. I couldn't make you happy anymore."

"Don't hate me."

"I don't."

She closed her eyes. "Tell Tracy I'm sorry and I will always love her."

"I think she knows that."

The monitor suddenly let out a high-pitched steady tone.

A nurse came rushing in and ordered him to leave the room. Dr. Grant ran in behind her as Parker stumbled out the door watching in disbelief as they tried without success to revive her.

While Parker sat outside the room, holding his daughter, he thought back to the times that were good between him and Lynn, to the days when they were happy. They seemed a lifetime ago.

Now he would start a new life with his daughter, try to make up for all the lost years—if only time and fate were on his side.

Chapter 26

Phillip walked Mike to the door of his office. "Thanks for everything," he said, extending his hand.

Mike turned at the threshold. "It's my job. I hope the information helps you and Vikki. You sure you don't want me to be there when you tell her?"

"No." Phillip shook his head. "It's better that I do this alone. She doesn't even know that I hired you."

"What? If Vikki is still the same woman I remember, she is going to have a fit. You might need me there to protect you."

Phillip gave a short laugh. "You might be right, but I'll take my chances."

"Okay. But if you need anything else let me know. Everything is contained in the paperwork in that folder."

"Right. Thanks again, buddy."

"No problem."

"Tell Leslie I said hello," Phillip called out to his departing friend.

"Will do."

Phillip closed the door to his office and returned to his desk. Sitting down, he flipped open the folder containing Mike's notes, official documents, and photographs.

He picked up the picture on the top. "So this is where Victoria gets that smile," he said aloud. "And there's your determined chin," he noted, looking at the second photograph.

Thoughtfully, he closed the folder. When he'd gotten the call from Mike telling him he'd found Vikki's family, there was a part of him that was relieved that some of the questions would finally be answered. But the reality remained; what if this discovery was worse than not knowing? How would they respond to each other?

He'd struggled with the whole notion of telling her at all, until this very moment. Looking at the photographs sealed it for him.

All of Victoria's life she'd spent hating herself, hating how she looked and pretending otherwise. Her self-loathing went so deep that she never wanted to have children as a result, married him, a white man, as if that would somehow absolve her of her blackness. Her unexpected pregnancy, in her mind, was a tragedy instead of a blessing.

If he didn't love her as much as he did, he would have walked away. But he knew that beneath the veneer that Victoria wrapped around herself was a wounded soul that desperately wanted to be healed.

All he could do was hope that discovering and accepting her true beginnings would help in that self-awareness.

His private line buzzed.

"Yes, Caitlyn?"

"They're waiting for you in the conference room."

He squeezed his eyes shut. "Thanks. I'll be right in."

He'd been so overwhelmed by the revelations made by Mike that he'd totally forgotten he was supposed to be in a meeting ten minutes earlier. In addition to the fact that he knew this meeting was going to take up the rest of the day, he wasn't looking forward to it. The committee had already been put on notice that dinner was going to be ordered in. He pushed papers aside on his desk and found the folder he was looking for, tucked it under his arm, and hurried out.

"If my wife calls, please tell her that I'll be very late tonight and I'll call when I can."

"Yes, Mr. Hunter." She watched him hurry off and her pleasant expression melted like butter on a skillet.

Caitlyn Singleton had worked for Phillip Hunter as his personal assistant for more than fifteen years. Every decision, every move he made she knew of and had input on, everything but his marriage to Victoria.

When he confided in her that he was getting married, one afternoon over a business lunch in the conference room, she nearly choked on her veal parmesan.

She'd taken a sip of her mineral water and forced herself to smile. "That's . . . wonderful. Congratulations." She started to feel sick inside.

"Thanks. She's a wonderful woman. I know we're going to be very happy."

"I didn't know you were . . . seeing anyone," she

managed, then hid the pain in her eyes behind her lowered lids. She shoved a forkful of food into her mouth.

He shrugged and flushed slightly. "We, uh, kind of kept our relationship private."

The more he talked about this wonderful Victoria and the plans that they were making together the more anguish she felt. How could this have happened? Couldn't Phillip see how much she cared about him, that she would do anything for him? She loved him in silence and at a distance for years, afraid to cross that invisible employer/employee line. This was what it had cost her.

It wasn't until Phillip brought in his wedding pictures that Caitlyn understood why he'd kept his relationship out of view. She was black, and not just brown—black.

For weeks she could barely sleep imagining him making love to his black wife and wondering if all the myths about black women being insatiable were true. Many mornings she would come to work and think about quitting, not knowing if she could stand to look at him and know that he was sleeping with someone else every night. But what would have been worse was not seeing Phillip at all. So she stayed and loved him in silence.

The buzzing intercom jerked her back to reality. She pressed the flashing button.

"Mr. Hunter's office."

"Caitlyn, it's me. I need you to bring me the Louis file. It's in the second drawer under my desk. Make sure it's the merger file, not the portfolio."

"Right away, Mr. Hunter."

Caitlyn pushed up from her desk and went into her boss's office. The first thing that hit her when

she stepped inside was that she was going to have
to get in there and straighten things out again. Mr.
Hunter might be a brilliant broker and analyst,
but when it came to organization he left a lot to be
desired. She teased him about it repeatedly when
his files and folders went missing. He insisted that
there was a method to his madness, but neither of
them could figure out what that was.

She crossed the carpeted office and went behind
his desk to get into the file drawers located beneath.
Of course the drawer was jammed as usual, and
when she tugged it open the vibration sent the
folders and loose papers on top of the desk onto
the floor.

"Damn."

She quickly rifled through the overstuffed file
drawer, more determined than ever to get the office in shape. She found the file she needed and
pulled it out. Forcing the drawer shut, she got up,
stepped over and around the debris she'd created,
and hustled down to the conference room.

When Caitlyn returned she went straight to
Phillip's office. For a moment she stood in the doorway taking in the chaos. It would take hours to sort
things out, but at least by the time he was finished
with his meeting, the office would be in some semblance of order.

With determination in her step she headed
straight for the desk. In her mind the desk was like
a bed. It was the centerpiece of the room. When
that was messy everything looked messy.

She began with the top of the desk and put everything on the floor along with what she'd knocked
over earlier. File by file, paper by paper, she put
everything in appropriate stacks, then began putting

them away. When she reached the bottom she
picked up the last folder and realized that it wasn't
a company folder at all. She started to set it in
Phillip's chair when she noticed the edge of a photograph sticking out.

Caitlyn glanced toward the door even though
she knew it was closed. She slipped the picture out
of the folder and held it up in front of her. It was a
worn photograph of a woman sitting on a dilapi-
dated porch. She stared at the smiling face of the
woman who looked very much like Phillip's wife.

Taking the file, she sat down and carefully went
through the contents, reading each and every word,
absorbing all the information. Everything that Victoria Hunter presented herself to be was a lie. She
didn't come from a high-class Atlanta-bred family,
far from it.

Caitlyn shoved the information back into the
folder. She didn't know how she could use this information, but there had to be some way to make
it work to her advantage. Maybe Phillip would finally see Victoria for who she really was—someone
not worthy of him. Caitlyn would make him see
that once and for all.

Chapter 27

"You have a visitor," the nurse said to Toni as she adjusted the sheets around her patient.

"Thank you." Toni sat up and tried to brush down her hair with her hands. She looked up as Alan walked in, and suddenly she wished she hadn't called him.

Alan approached, his expression one of sadness mixed with relief that she wasn't as bad as his imagination had led him to believe.

"Hi," he said softly.

Toni reached out and touched his hand. "Thank you for coming."

"I'm just glad you're all right, Toni."

She chuckled without humor. "All right? I'm far from all right. If I was I wouldn't be here."

"You know what I mean."

"I know, I'm sorry."

Alan pulled up a chair and sat. "Why, Toni? Why would you try to hurt yourself?"

Toni lowered her gaze, trying to find the words

to explain what was going on in her heart and mind, what brought her to this point. She inhaled deeply and slowly let the words flow.

"When you asked me the other night if Charles came back would I try again, would I let him back in my life, I told you I didn't know." She looked him in the eye. "But I do know. I'm still very much in love with my husband and always will be. I'm sure he won't take me back. In fact I know he won't. He brought divorce papers for me to sign." Her eyes filled with tears, but she didn't cry. "I think when I saw them I finally understood what a fool I'd been, what I'd destroyed. I care about you, Alan, and always will, but I won't lead you on. I don't want you to think that, even now, with Charles gone for good, things could work out between us. It would never be fair to you.

"You are an incredible man, a loving man who deserves someone who can love you back without reservations. I know now that woman isn't me."

"Is that why you tried to hurt yourself, because of the divorce papers?"

"I felt so worthless, like such a failure and that nothing else mattered."

"Toni. If there was one thing you taught me in all the sessions we had, it's that you can't base your happiness on someone else."

"That advice always sounds good until it's you," she said, her voice heavy with regret. "I want you to be happy, Alan. I'll find my way."

He reached out and gently brushed her hair away from her face. "I know you will, sweetheart. And no matter what, I'll always be there for you if you ever need someone to talk to or just want to have a cup of coffee with." He forced a smile, then leaned down and tenderly kissed her on the forehead. "You take care of yourself."

"You too."

He turned to face Charles.

For a moment the two men who loved the same woman faced each other with recognition dawning in their eyes.

Charles looked beyond Alan to Toni, whose eyes seemed to beg him, for what he was uncertain.

"What are you doing here? Haven't you caused enough damage?" Charles snarled, the old wounds opening wide.

"I'm here because Toni asked me to come. But it's you she wants. And if you let her go, you're a fool."

Alan turned one last time to look at Toni, then walked out.

Charles stood there, unwilling to go near her. He slung his hands in his pockets. "Would I be a fool, Toni, to let you go?"

Her throat tightened, ached. "I'm the fool. I lost you and I have no one to blame but me. Then I did the ultimate foolish thing and tried to take the coward's way out instead of dealing with the woman that I am. I don't blame you for . . ." Her voice broke. "Not loving me."

Charles flexed his jaw. "That's just it . . . I do love you. That's why it hurts so fucking bad."

She held out her arms, praying that he would relent and walk into them.

It seemed as if the world came to a standstill, then began to move in slow motion as Charles took cautious steps toward her.

And then he was there beside her, holding her and letting her hold him. He whispered again and again his love for her as she did with him. She promised to make it work, to work on herself. And he promised to give them a real chance and that he would be a real partner in their marriage.

As Toni held her husband and rejoiced in the possibility of the future, she prayed that Charles would be as willing to forget as well as forgive. But she knew only time would tell.

Phillip was exhausted by the time the meeting finally ended. Putting together any major corporate merger was always grueling, but this one was more taxing than most. The clients were like pit bulls who'd been primed for blood. And when they weren't going after each other they went after him and his team.

Yet, even as tired as he was, excitement gave him that last boost of energy. He glanced briefly at the passenger seat to the folder that had been given to him by Mike.

He knew Vikki would be upset by what he'd done without telling her, but what he'd found had been worth it. He was certain of that. He could do now what he had not been able to do in all the years of their marriage, give his wife her past so that she could finally have a future.

He parked the car in front of their house, took the folder and his briefcase, and got out.

When he stepped inside the house, all the lights on the ground floor were out, but he heard music coming from upstairs. Good, Vikki was still awake.

He hung his jacket up in the hall closet and hurried upstairs. When he stepped into the bedroom, Victoria was propped up in bed reading a magazine. She put it down and welcomed him with a smile.

"Hey," she said, "finally made it. Thought I was going to have to send the troops out for you."

Phillip laughed and loosened his tie. "I thought the same thing for a while. Rough day."

"Did you eat?"

"Yeah. I would rather have had dinner with you." He crossed the room and sat on the side of the bed next to her. He leaned over and kissed her, slow and sweet. "I love you," he said.

"I know." She noticed the folder that he'd set on the dresser. "Phil, please don't tell me you brought work home for the weekend. I'd hoped we could get out and do something."

He glanced at the folder, then back at Victoria. "No, it's not work. But it is something we need to talk about."

He got up from the bed and retrieved the folder, then came back and sat down next to his wife.

"Before you blow up at me, just please listen. . . ."

Phillip began telling Victoria about how he'd asked for Mike's help in finding out about her family.

"You did what! Why would you do something like that? I—"

Phillip grabbed her wrists. "Vikki, listen to me. I did it for you, for us. I found your real family."

For a minute he thought she would faint. He saw her draw in a ragged breath and not release it. Her eyes widened and she snatched her hands away from his grip.

"Wh-what are you saying . . . my real family?"

"Vikki, relax. The news is not bad, it's wonderful."

"What do you mean my real family?" she repeated.

"The woman that raised you, the sisters that you lived with all those years, were not your real family." He pulled out the documents from the folder and spread them on the bed. He lifted a photograph from the pile. "This is your real mother."

"No."

"She is, sweetheart, and she wants to meet you. You have a real sister, too. Your mother's name is Ellen Lawry and your father's name is William. Your sister's name is Felicia and you have a niece."

She shook her head back and forth. "That can't be true." She knocked all the papers to the floor and glared at him. "Why would you tell me these lies? Why?"

"They're not lies, Victoria. It's the truth. Your mother became pregnant with you when she was only fifteen. Her father, your grandfather, was a minister and he refused to let her keep the child and cause a scandal in his congregation. He sent her away to have you and forced your mother to give you up." He stroked her arm. "Your mother and father eventually married and had your sister, Felicia. They didn't know where to find you." He leaned down and picked up the photograph of her mother. "Look at it, Victoria. That's your face. Your beautiful face and smile. Those people who raised you taught you to hate yourself. They had no connection to you. But she does." He pointed to the picture. "Take it, look at it." He pushed the photograph into her hand.

With great reluctance Victoria took the picture and turned wary eyes on the face that so resembled her own. It was almost like looking in the mirror, seeing a reflection of herself, something she'd never been able to do. When she looked in the mirror all she'd ever seen was ugliness, the ugliness that had been put into her head all her life. Her lips trembled as her throat worked up and down trying to form words.

"Our baby can have a real family. A family that will love it and you," he said gently. "And no one is more deserving of love than you are."

"All these years," she said, the ache apparent in her voice. "All these years of believing the things they said to me, and my real family was out there somewhere."

"Your mother wants to hear from you. She wants to see you."

"Are you sure?" she said, sounding like a child.

Phillip smiled and brushed her hair with his hand. "Yes, I'm sure, whenever you're ready."

She swallowed over the knot in her throat. "I . . . What if I'm not what they expect?" She looked at him with an imploring gaze.

"That's not possible," he said simply. "They will love you as much as I do." He gathered her in his arms and held her close as she cried softly against his chest. But this time he was certain they were tears of joy.

Chapter 28

"Thanks for opening the store for me, Renee," Regina said as she approached the counter. She stepped around it and put her purse beneath the shelf.

"No problem." Renee paused and looked at Regina. "Are you okay, Ms. Everette? You look . . . I don't know . . . upset or something."

Regina tried to keep her hands from shaking as she took off her jacket. She kept her gaze averted. "No. I'm fine."

The bell over the door chimed and a customer walked in.

"Why don't you go take care of our first customer for the day while I get settled?" She walked away and headed for the back room.

Once behind closed doors she collapsed in the first available chair. She was shaking like a leaf. She probably should have gone home after her doctor's visit, but she didn't want to be questioned by the kids as to why she was home when she normally would have been at work.

The kids. Her life. What would she do if the tests came back positive? Dread swept through her. The nurse said it would take two to three days for the results to be returned. How was she going to get through the next few days?

No matter how many times she ran the scenario through her head she couldn't comprehend why this had happened. She'd been so sure about her and Parker. He was the only man other than her husband that she'd ever slept with, and for all of Russell's arrogance, macho behavior, and often selfish attitude, never once did he put her life in jeopardy. The one time when she decided to let go and turn her heart and emotions over to someone else—this happened.

A wave of nausea rolled through her stomach and she had to take deep gulps of air to fight it back. She hadn't been able to eat or sleep since Parker's phone call, not to mention the visit by Kelly. There'd been no one she could turn to, no one to share her terror and ease her fears. Toni was hospitalized with her own drama and she wouldn't dare lay this in Victoria's lap, she was already in a fragile state. So she had to keep her own counsel and pray. And Russell, to his credit, was good at his word. When he said he was going to do everything he could to win her back, that's exactly what he meant.

He'd been calling her every day, sometimes twice, "just to say hello," or to "let you know I was thinking about you." She came up with all kinds of excuses as to why she wouldn't see him, but her resolve was beginning to weaken. As bizarre as it was, Russell was the only friend she could turn to. She'd been on the verge of telling him everything last night when he called just before she went to bed. But she quickly thought better of it. She didn't want his sympathy or his anger unleashed.

Regina looked around. She couldn't very well sit in this room all day, she realized. But she didn't know if she could get through the day smiling and being polite for hours when her head and her life were in turmoil.

Then again, maybe keeping herself occupied would help, at least for a little while.

Sighing deeply, she got up and went back to the front of the store. Renee was on the phone and there were several customers browsing the shelves. Regina put on her best smile and went to assist her customers.

While she was helping a young woman find a book for her son, Renee came up to her.

"Ms. Everette," she whispered. "I need to leave. Family emergency."

Regina frowned in concern. "Is there anything I can do?"

"No. It's my mom's asthma again. My sister took her to the hospital and wants me to meet her over there."

Regina put her hand on Renee's shoulder. "Sure. Go, go. I hope your mom will be okay."

"Thanks." She hurried away.

Regina went back to her customer. Now she didn't have any other choice but to get her act and her head together, she mused as she selected a Walter Dean Meyers book for the young woman. She had at least another six hours to go before her workday came to an end. Hopefully it wouldn't get too hectic.

That hope quickly flew out the window when an out-of-town book club with more than twenty members descended on the store. They were visiting as many small black bookstores in New York as they could, the club's president said, and Regina's Place was on their list.

Regina gave them the grand tour and they were duly impressed with her extensive inventory and particularly impressed with the exquisite artwork that she had on display.

"Who is the artist?" one woman asked.

Regina could barely say his name. "Parker Heywood."

"Great stuff," the woman commented. "I think I might pick up a piece or two. I love art."

Regina pressed her lips together in a tight smile. "Well, take a look and let me know what you decide."

"Thanks, I will."

As people are prone to do, when they see a crowd they immediately want to know what's going on, thinking that they might be missing something. Before Regina knew it, the store was packed. She couldn't ring up the purchases fast enough. The little café set up in the back of the shop where she served tea, coffee, and muffins was at capacity and folks were actually waiting to be seated. She darted back and forth like a squirrel after nuts trying to keep everyone happy and an eye on her inventory at the same time.

Under any other circumstances she would have loved this challenge, but today was not the day.

When the bell over the door rang again, she

wanted to scream until she saw who it was. She was actually relieved.

"Wow. Are you giving things away today?" Russell joked as he took in the parade of people.

"Looks that way."

"Where's Renee?"

"She had to leave, family emergency."

His brows rose. "You're here by yourself?"

"Yeah."

The corner of his mouth lifted up in a crooked smile. "Then I guess taking you to lunch is out."

"I guess," she deadpanned.

Russell took off his coat and suit jacket. "Where can I put these?"

Regina frowned. "Huh?"

"Where can I put these?"

"In the back," she said absently.

Russell walked off to the back of the store to the small office and quickly returned. "What do you need me to do?"

"What?"

He angled his head. "Are you having hearing problems today? What do you need me to do?"

She blinked rapidly, then finally put together what he was saying. "Uh, can you work the café?"

"Sure. I used to wait tables in college." He winked at her and headed toward the café.

Regina shook her head in amazement, certain that this was some bizarre dream. But if it was, it sure was a noisy dream.

The day sped by and Regina and Russell worked side by side. He was as good at taking instructions as he was at giving them. In no time he'd mastered the computer system to account for the sales. He charmed all the women who set foot in the place, and if Regina didn't know better she'd swear that the line in the café continued just so that they could be served by Russell. It was all a mind-altering experience. She watched him interact with the customers, smiling and joking, charming everyone. And for the first time in longer than she could remember she saw Russell with new eyes. Perhaps this was the man everyone else saw, whom the world saw and whom she'd been blinded to for a variety of reasons that at the moment were totally unclear to her.

By closing time, Regina thought she was going to have to start flashing the lights the way they do in nightclubs to get the folks to finally leave. It was Russell who escorted everyone to the door, often carrying packages to their cars and encouraging them to come back.

When he closed the door behind the last customer and locked it, he turned to her with the biggest grin on his face.

"That was fun."

In that moment it seemed as if all the weight were suddenly lifted off her and she broke out in laughter, releasing all the tension that had held her in a knot for days.

"You call that fun?" she said, still chuckling.

"Absolutely. Nothing like a challenge to get the old juices flowing. I actually had a good time."

He walked toward her and leaned against the counter. "What's left to do?"

She looked around at her displays. "Well," she said

on a breath, "I need to straighten out the racks and the shelves for tomorrow, tally up the receipts, and make a deposit at the bank."

"What do you need me to do?"

"You can work the shelves while I check what supplies I have left in the café."

"Done."

"Want some coffee?" she called out.

"Sure."

She put on a fresh pot and was surprised to hear Russell humming as he worked. She smiled.

"So," Russell began as they stood outside the store. "Where's your bank?"

"Two blocks down." Regina set the store alarm and checked the gate.

"Wanna walk? It's still nice out."

"Okay."

They headed down Fulton Street walking in companionable silence. The evening was quite lovely. The sky was clear and there was a warm breeze, the first sign that spring was on its way out and summer was not far behind. Even at seven-thirty, the sun still hung precariously in the sky.

Regina stopped in front of Citibank and put her pouch in the night depository slot. She turned to Russell, who stood like a sentinel behind her.

"All done," she said. "Thanks for today."

"It was my pleasure. Really."

"I never asked you, but what were you doing down here anyway?"

"Took the day off. I had some time coming to me. I thought I would surprise you and/or you would surprise me and let me take you to lunch." He shrugged. "But business got in the way."

"Still hungry?" she asked, startling herself with the question.

Russell grinned. "Starved is more like it. There's only so much coffee and muffins I can take. Is that an offer?"

"Something like that."

"Where would you like to go?"

"There's a great Italian restaurant in Brooklyn Heights. Armandos."

"I remember," he said. "We went there on one of our first dates." He looked down at her and the memory was reflected in her eyes.

"Still want to go?" she asked, toying with levity.

"Yeah, let's go, for old times' sake. Did you drive?"

"No." She didn't want to tell him that her nerves had been too frazzled to attempt to drive today.

"I'm parked around the corner." He placed his hand at the small of her back as they walked back toward his car.

Over dinner it seemed as if all the years of ugliness disappeared, if only for the moment. They shared wine and old war stories of their early days together—at least the good times.

"Remember when your mother first invited me over to the house?" Russell asked over a mouthful of linguine.

Regina chuckled. "I was pissed and scared silly that she'd set me up."

"You were so cute, barely said a word."

"I think I was overly impressed with you."

"Overly impressed? Did I at least live up to expectations?"

"Definitely. I suppose I just wondered what you saw in me, to be truthful."

He put down his fork. "What I saw was a young woman who wanted to bloom but didn't know how. I saw someone with incredible potential. I guess I took on the cause of trying to make you be the woman I thought you should be instead of who you really were inside."

"And what was that?"

He hesitated for a moment. "Someone who needed to find her way on her own, in her own time. Someone who needed the support of those around her to accomplish her goals instead of beating them down. And I think over time it scared me," he admitted.

"You, scared?"

"Yeah. The more you struggled to be strong and independent the more I thought I was losing you, so I just went into my macho arsenal to stop it."

Regina looked down at her plate.

"I'm sorry."

She looked up.

"I'm sorry for all the stupid things I did wrong. I'm sorry for not being there for you, for not believing in you. I screwed up and I've been regretting it every day since."

"I think about those days too—sometimes," she qualified. "I wonder how I could have been different. But sometimes I felt as if I was suffocating."

"I know."

"What went wrong between us was as much my fault as yours because I allowed you to treat me the way that you did. I didn't want to rock the boat."

"What about now, Regina, are you happy? I mean really happy—with—him?"

That was the last question she wanted to answer. "Parker and I . . . are having our problems right now . . . but . . ."

"But?"

"We'll work them out," she stated flatly, not even sure if that was a possibility any longer.

"And if they don't?"

"What are you asking me, Russell?"

"If things don't work out . . . what about us?"

"Russell—"

He held up his hand. "Forget it. Don't answer that. It was unfair of me to ask. That was my ego talking." He forced a smile. "Eat up. Your food is getting cold."

Russell pulled up in front of her house in Canarsie. "Thanks for tonight."

She smiled. "Thanks for today. Don't know how I would have handled it if you hadn't come in."

"Anytime. Now that I have the hang of it." He turned to her. "You should be proud of yourself. I am."

"Thanks." She unbuckled her seat belt. "Well, I better get upstairs."

"Yeah," he said somberly, then without warning leaned over and pulled her to him.

He kissed her long and gentle, pouring out his heart in a tender kiss that stirred her soul as much as she fought against it.

Without thinking she gave in to the taste of his mouth, the familiar brush of his tongue, the strong arms that held her in a protective embrace. And suddenly the wall that she'd built around her heart to shield her emotions from Russell seemed to crumble.

The pain and confusion that she'd experienced in the past few days took their final toll and she couldn't be strong any longer, she didn't want to be. What she wanted was to be taken care of, to have the pain go away and be replaced with pleasure.

Russell moaned against her mouth even as his hand roamed freely across her breasts, setting off shock waves of desire in them both.

"I want you, Gina. Come home with me. Say yes."

Reality abruptly joined them in the confines of the car. What was she doing? As much as she needed to feel the pleasures of a man, she knew she couldn't do this, not now—especially not now. Russell didn't deserve to be put at risk.

She pulled away. "Russell, I can't. This isn't right. You know it isn't."

He was breathing hard, his eyes dark with longing. "You still want me. Admit it."

She looked at him with a hard stare. "Is that what this is really about, seeing if you can get me back in bed with you?" she asked, incredulity raising the octave of her voice.

"It was always great between us. You know it was and it can be again."

"So all this talk about you being sorry and how you messed up it was all bull." She popped open the lock and pushed the door open.

Russell reached for her and missed. He jumped out of the car from his side and cut her off in front.

"Gina, wait. That's not what I meant."

"Let go of me, Russell."

He dropped her arm and stepped back. "Gina, just listen. That was pure lust talking, and it will make me say and act the fool in a minute. But it doesn't change how I feel. This was not about getting you in bed . . . well, maybe just a little." He hoped that would make her smile, but it didn't. "I meant everything I said tonight and have been saying."

"Fine. I'm going upstairs. Good night, Russell."

Russell let out a breath and stepped back, allowing her to pass.

She walked to her front door on shaky legs.

"I meant what I said, Gina," he called out.

Regina hesitated for an instant before putting her key in the lock. She opened the door and shut it without ever looking back.

Chapter 29

Parker opened the door to his loft and stepped aside to let his daughter pass.

"This is it," he said, bringing her suitcases in behind her.

Tracy stepped inside and looked around without comment.

"I figured you could have the bedroom. I can bunk out on the couch until . . . well, until we can work something else out." He had yet to figure out that part of the equation.

In a matter of days both of their lives had gone through a major upheaval. It had taken hours of talking from both him and a hospital social worker to get Tracy to accept that the best place for her at the time was with her father.

The private memorial service for Lynn had been traumatic at best. Tracy had been almost inconsolable, then utterly stoic. Since that morning three days earlier, she hadn't shed a tear or said another word about it. She barely spoke unless asked a direct question.

The social worker advised him that it would take a while for her to adjust and suggested that he seek counseling for her when they got back to New York. She was going to need his attention and assurance that he wouldn't leave her as well, as she struggled through issues of feeling abandoned by her mother.

He wasn't sure how they were going to pull through it all, but he was going to give it all he had. He made a vow that he would never shortchange his daughter again.

"Let me show you your room," he said, putting his arm around her stiff shoulder. He guided her down the corridor to the bedroom. He opened the door and could have kicked himself. There hanging above the bed, as big as life, was his rendition of a nude Regina.

Tracy stared up at the picture, then seemed to ignore it. She walked to the bed, reached for the remote on the nightstand, and turned on the television, totally dismissing him.

"I'll bring your bags and you can get settled. I just have to move some things around."

She stared at the television.

Parker hesitated in the doorway for a moment, thinking he should say something, but he didn't know what. He turned and walked out.

Standing alone in the front room, he had a moment to absorb the enormity of his new situation. He'd no longer have the luxury of coming and going as he wished. He'd have to find a school for

Tracy, which was going to be difficult as they were coming to the end of the school year. Not to mention finding a counselor for her.

He sat down on the couch. Those were surface things compared to what lay at the heart of it all. He needed to get the test results as soon as possible. With all that was going on in California he didn't take time to go back. But he couldn't put it off. He needed to know.

He glanced at the phone on the table against the wall. He wanted to call Regina, hear her voice, and just let her know that he was home and that they *were* going to talk.

Kelly was another issue. That had been a stupid, senseless move on his part. Never go back, his buddies in college had always cautioned.

He'd met Kelly about five years earlier at an art exhibit hosted by Pratt Institute. He thought she was kind of cute in a campy sort of way, funny and intelligent enough to hold a good conversation. He'd been alone for a while and Kelly seemed more than interested and available.

He never pretended that he wanted a permanent relationship and she didn't seem interested in one either. In other words, they used each other to satisfy whatever need required scratching at the moment.

It was fine for a while between them, until Kelly decided she wanted a real relationship, something he knew he couldn't give her. So they went their separate ways, and then he met Regina.

Everything was great between them. From the moment he met her he knew she was the one he was destined to spend the rest of his life with. But then came the problems with the kids and the tension between them.

He'd been at a bar one night, drowning his annoyance. He hadn't been able to spend time with Regina in weeks and wondered just how much longer she was going to keep him at bay, and then Kelly walked in.

After sharing small talk and several drinks he wound up at her house. Mistake number one, going back. The second was apparently not scratching what itched her.

Instead, he told her all about Regina and how much he cared about her, and because he did he couldn't sleep with her no matter how lovely and desirable she was. He'd said his good-byes and he hadn't seen her since.

Where and how had Regina run into Kelly? He rubbed his hands over his face, debating whether he should call her now or if he should wait. It was better if he saw her in person, he decided. At least she wouldn't be able to hang up on him. But before he did that he was going to have the test results back. At least then he would know what he was dealing with. He picked up the phone.

Regina locked up the register and got her purse.

"Do you need a ride, Renee?"

"No, thanks, Ms. Everette. I'm going to meet my sister downtown for dinner."

"Okay. Ready?"

Renee took a last look around. "Yep."

"How is your mother doing these days?" Regina asked as she set the alarm and locked the door.

"Much better. Her asthma is brought on by stress and she refuses to stop worrying about every- and anything. If I'm five minutes late getting home from school or work she starts worrying."

Regina laughed softly to herself. She did the same thing with her kids, she thought.

"Unfortunately, that's part of a mother's job. I think it's in our genes."

"I guess. Well, good night. See you tomorrow."

"Have a good evening and don't forget to call your mom if you're going to be late."

Renee laughed. "I will."

Regina walked the half block to where her car was parked. Just the brief conversation with Renee and the whole mother, child relationship thing made her realize that since Parker had been away Michele seemed like a different person. She wasn't sure if she should attribute her daughter's change in behavior solely to Parker's absence or the talk they'd had. She also supposed that Russell's presence in their lives on a more regular basis didn't hurt either.

Russell had definitely taken a step back since the night in the car, she mused. He still called every day, but the calls weren't laced with propositions. She wasn't sure if she was relieved or disappointed.

She looked both ways before unlocking her car, a precaution that Parker had advised her of when they'd first met. You can never be too careful, he'd said, especially a woman getting into a car alone at night.

It had been more than a week since the last time she heard from Parker. She had no idea where he was or if he'd ever come back. Since getting her negative test results the day before, she was breathing a little easier, but as the doctor indicated, she still needed to be tested every six months for the next two years—just to be sure.

Regina opened the car door, just as she heard her name being called. She looked up and across the street.

Parker.

Chapter 30

Regina felt her heart begin to race as she watched Parker cross the street. She wanted to jump in her car and tear away from the curb, then she wanted to slap him for the torture he'd put her through, and on top of it all she wanted to hold him and have him hold her, swearing to her that everything would be okay. All these emotions swirled through her in a matter of seconds, battling with each other for dominance.

"Hi," he said softly. "I didn't want to come into the store, so I waited for you to leave."

Regina put her hand on her hip. "What do you want, Parker? I think we've said all we have to say to each other."

"No, we haven't. We haven't nearly said it all. At least I know I haven't."

She reached for the door handle. He grabbed her hand.

"Don't run off, Gina," he said, his voice even and deathly calm. "That's not going to solve anything.

And if I know you at all, you want to hear what I have to say."

"You have two minutes and the clock is ticking."

"First of all, I don't know what Kelly told you but I haven't slept with her in nearly five years, long before I met you. I ran into her about a month ago. Yeah, I wound up at her house, sitting on her couch, slightly drunk, and all I talked about was you." He stared her straight in the eye. "I don't know what she told you, but whatever it is, it's a lie."

"She said she's pregnant."

He made a noise in his throat. "She might be, but unless she's aiming for the Guinness book of records for the longest pregnancy on record—it's not mine."

Regina pursed her lips. "That's the least of it, Parker."

"I know and that's what we need to talk about, Gina."

"Your two minutes are up." She opened the car door.

"The test was negative."

She stopped and turned. "So was mine."

Relief washed over him. "Can we go somewhere and talk? I won't take up too much of your time. I know you need to get home to the kids and I need to get back to Tracy."

She hesitated a moment. "We can walk down to the park," she finally said.

"Fine."

Parker started to take her arm the way he always did, but she pulled away and walked a bit faster. They walked toward the park in silence, like two strangers who had nothing in common except the same destination.

When they entered Ft. Greene Park, Regina pointed out a bench beneath a tree that was just beginning to bloom. The sun was setting and the atmosphere was tranquil. A few strollers meandered down the lanes, while others walked their dogs.

The park had come a long way from the days of her youth, Regina thought absently as she sat down. It had once been notorious for drugs and gang violence. Now it was a centerpiece of the neighborhood.

"I'm listening," she said without preamble.

Parker cleared his throat. He'd thought talking about what had transpired would be easier, that it would flow right from him, but it didn't. It was still hard to put the words together.

"Lynn died a week ago," he said, the pain still evident in his voice. "We, uh, had a memorial service."

Regina didn't respond. Anything she could have said would sound trite. A million questions raced through her head, but she let them rest and let him speak.

By degrees, he poured out the story of his and Lynn's relationship, her meeting Paul and leaving him.

"She said that she caught the virus from Paul. He died a year ago." He turned to look at her, but she continued to stare straight ahead. "We weren't together then, but she had been intimate with him toward the end of our marriage, that's why I took the test." He took her hand and was relieved when she didn't pull away. "I didn't know, Gina. I would never do anything to jeopardize you. You have to know that."

She didn't respond.

Parker tugged in a deep breath. "I have never been unfaithful to you. Never."

She thought about the kiss she shared with Russell and the night in his car when her anger and hurt almost got the best of her. Guilt knocked in her chest.

"I know," she finally said. "This has all been a nightmare."

"For me too. But we can work through it, together. We can. I'm willing if you are."

Slowly she turned to him. "How is your daughter?"

He shook his head. "Not good. She's taken it very hard. The social worker at the hospital suggested that I get her into counseling as soon as possible. Do you think that Toni would see her? I don't know anyone else."

"Hmmm. Toni is in need of some counseling herself right now." She paused. "She tried to kill herself."

"What?"

Regina told him what happened.

"Wow. How is she now?"

"Better. She's supposed to come home tomorrow."

"I'm really sorry. She seemed so together, you know. Even after . . . the thing with her and her husband."

"That's what I thought, too. But I suppose all of us have something in our closets that no one else knows about."

He took the barb in stride. "I'm sorry," he said. "Sorry that you had to go through any of this. And I'm sorry that I wasn't here with you."

"I'm a big girl." The corner of her mouth curved. "I'm not as fragile as I look."

"So I see." He glanced down. "What do you want to do—about us?"

"I've really been rocked by all this, Parker. I don't think I've ever been so hurt and confused—even when I was going through all the changes with Russell." She turned and looked him in the eye. "And the reason why all this has messed with me so much is that . . . I'm in love with you."

The breath caught in his chest. She'd never said the words to him. Never. Although she'd always been kind and loving and considerate, she'd never admitted her true feelings.

Parker reached out and cupped her chin. "I love you, too, Gina. From the bottom of my heart I love you. I know we can do this. We can beat anything if we do it together." His eyes roamed over her face, searching for acceptance of his declaration.

Her throat tightened and her heart raced with the fear of stepping into more unknown territory. It was one thing to contemplate love and all of its ramifications in your head, but to say the words aloud to that person made it real.

"One day at a time," she said on a breath of hope.

"Yes," he said, holding her fast with his gaze. "Can I kiss you, Gina?"

She gave the slightest of nods.

Regina watched him as he slowly leaned toward her, his eyes never leaving hers even as his lips touched hers with a tenderness that made her heart ache with happiness. His was a kiss filled with truth and promise. She knew that now and she parted her lips to taste him. This was not a kiss filled with lust and ego, like what she'd shared with Russell. It was one that was a testament to their love for each other. Not a kiss of the past, it was a pathway to their future, a stamp on their commitment.

If she was going to truly love him, open her heart to him, she was going to have to continue to examine her inner self and be true to her heart. She was going to have to be willing to share her life, her thoughts and emotions—totally—and most of all she was going to have to trust Parker to do the same—one day at a time.

By degrees they parted, and reflected in their eyes were mirror images of the same understanding. It was not going to be easy. There was never anything easy about love. But if they put their minds and hearts to it, they could at least get over a lot of the obstacles that were in front of them. And if some of the obstacles tripped them up, they would still stand tall together.

"I guess we better get back to the kids," Parker said softly.

Regina smiled. "Yeah. I guess. When can I meet your daughter?"

"Maybe we can plan something for the weekend with all the kids. Tracy will definitely need some friends."

"And some mothering," Regina added. "We'll work it out."

"I like the sound of that. *We.*"

"So do I."

Parker took her hand and they stood, then began walking back to Regina's car.

Although they walked in companionable silence, they were both wrapped in contemplation. Talking was the easy part. Making their ideals a reality was a completely different story. And they knew that this first step was only the beginning. The real battle lay ahead.

Chapter 31

"Your husband is here to pick you up, Mrs. Devon," the nurse said.

Toni buttoned the bottom button of her blouse. "I'm ready," she said.

In the days that she'd been in the hospital, she'd had plenty of time to think about not only what she'd done but what she needed to do. She'd allowed the weight of life to beat her down. She'd allowed her emotions to control her life and she'd almost lost it as a result. Deep inside she knew she was better than that, stronger than that.

She'd pulled herself up from a life of poverty, ignorance, and illiteracy to build a career, a home, a family. Sure, none of it was perfect, but she'd done it. She'd beaten the odds that said she'd never make it. But she had and she would beat this as well.

Toni got down off the side of the bed when Charles and Steven walked into the room. Seeing her son made her heart break all over again. Her self-absorption had nearly ruined him and almost lost his mother in the process. How could she have been so selfish to do that to him?

She held her arms out to him.

Tentatively, Steven walked forward and stepped into her embrace. She held him with all the strength in her body.

"I'm so sorry, sweetheart. So sorry."

"I love you, Mom."

She felt his body shudder and she held him tighter. "I love you too, baby." She stepped back, quickly wiped her eyes, and forced a smile. "We're going to be okay." She put her arm around his shoulder and faced Charles. "Thanks for coming."

He nodded. "Ready?"

"Yes."

Victoria decided to surprise Phillip and take him to lunch. After she'd gotten over the shock of what he'd done, she realized that deep inside it was what she'd spent her life searching for—validation from the people who loved her. Now she understood why there was no connection between the woman who raised her and the two girls she believed were her sisters. Perhaps if they'd told her the truth from the beginning, she would not have spent so many years hating herself. What they'd done to her, to her spirit, was unforgivable and cruel. But just as she'd gotten through all the other trials in her life, she'd get over this too.

It was still a frightening concept to actually meet her real family, she thought as she got off the elevator on Phillip's office floor. But she knew that Phillip was in her corner.

Victoria approached his assistant Caitlyn's desk.

"Hi, Caitlyn. Is Phillip in his office? I wanted to surprise him and take him to lunch."

Caitlyn stared in disbelief at her protruding belly. Phillip was having a baby with *her!* She cleared her throat.

"Mr. Hunter is in a meeting. I'll be sure to tell him you stopped by."

Victoria frowned. "Is he in a meeting out of the office?" she asked, taken aback by Caitlyn's caustic tone.

"No. He's in the conference room and I have no idea how long he will be."

Victoria straightened her shoulders. "I'll wait in his office. I'm sure he won't mind."

Caitlyn stood. "Mr. Hunter doesn't like anyone in his office, except me. You're free to have a seat in the waiting room."

Victoria put her hand on her hip and looked this crazy woman up and down.

"I beg your pardon. I think you must have me confused with someone else," she said with a snap of her neck.

"No, I think Phillip has *you* confused with someone else."

"Look, I don't know what your problem is, but—"

"The problem is you. You think I don't really know about you?" She smiled a nasty smile. "You're nobody, an illegitimate nobody who wants to pretend that she's someone! I saw the file. You don't deserve someone like Phillip."

Victoria was so stunned she couldn't speak for a moment.

Caitlyn tossed her blond head back and laughed. "Yes, just like I thought. It's all true."

Something from deep inside Victoria rose to the

surface in a roaring wave, and before she realized it she'd reared back and slapped Caitlyn so hard she knocked her back into her seat.

Victoria's eyes were blazing with all the outrage, slights, and insults that she'd received over the years. She braced her hands on Caitlyn's desk and spoke so low and chillingly that she held Caitlyn captive.

"I don't know who you think I am. But I'm Victoria Hunter, Phillip's wife, and proud of it. And I may not have had the privileged background that you did, but I'm more of and a better woman than you will ever dream of being. That's why you are sitting on your fat ass and I'm standing over you!" She smiled. "I'm going to find *my* husband."

Caitlyn didn't dare move. All she could do was hold her hand to the sting on her cheek.

Victoria turned away, and even though her heart was racing out of control and her legs felt as if they were going to give out, she hadn't felt that good in her entire life. She shook her shoulders and laughed inwardly. So that was what it felt like to put someone in check, something she'd always told herself she was "above" doing. As a result she'd spent her life walking around with that inner rage that steadily ate away at her. Not anymore.

She was Victoria Hunter and she wasn't taking crap from anyone ever again.

Toni, Charles, and Steven filed into the house. Toni looked at her "castle" with new eyes. This had never been a real home, she thought, just a showplace, and she'd been the ringmaster, never taking into account what her family really needed or wanted. Her concern had been confined to the superficiality of it all, her way of covering up her own shortcoming and poor beginnings. The joy and fun family memories had never been part of the design. That realization saddened her.

"Can I get you anything?" Charles asked, pulling her away from her thoughts.

She turned to him. "No. I'm fine. I think I'll go up and change."

Charles nodded.

Toni headed up the stairs to the bedroom and the first thing she saw was the divorce papers still propped up against the lamp. She crossed the room and picked them up, reached into the drawer beneath, and took out a pen. Without thinking further she signed her name.

Slowly she put the paper down and took a ragged breath. A chapter of her life was now over.

Charles had been kind and caring when he'd come to the hospital to see her. He'd even given her the glimmer of hope that they could pick up and begin again. But she felt that it was only an act of sympathy, an impassioned moment, and that they were both vainly holding on by their fingertips to what was left of the ruination of their marriage.

If she was ever going to get her act together she was going to have to start with a clean slate. The first step toward healing was to accept that something was wrong and to accept her role in it. She believed that she finally had.

Somehow she and Charles would work out the details of raising Steven jointly. He needed both of his parents. But he needed them whole, not bitter pieces that no longer fit. Steven didn't deserve that. And he was what was most important now.

She turned at the sound of the knock on the partially opened bedroom door.

"Mind if I come in?"

"Come on in."

Charles crossed the room and sat beside her. "Toni—"

She held up her hand. "Before you say anything, I want to tell you that I'm okay. Probably better than I have been in a long time." She forced a smile. "I guess I needed a reality check." She reached for the papers and handed them to him. "They're signed," she said.

Charles looked down at the documents in her hand, knowing that when he took them it would signal the end to more than sixteen years of marriage. With a heavy heart he took them from her and saw the light dim in her eyes.

"What are we going to do about Steven?"

Toni inhaled deeply, fighting to keep her voice even. "That's up to Steven. I know you'll be there for him and so will I."

"The house?"

She looked around, all the years they'd spent there—both good and bad—reflected in her expression. "We can sell it and use the money to fund Steven's college." She chuckled without humor. "I certainly don't need all this space by myself."

Charles momentarily turned away, pressing his lips tightly together. "Whatever you want," he said in a near whisper. He pushed himself up and stood. He looked down into her upturned face. "I better go. I'll take Steven with me so you can get some rest."

Toni wanted to grab his shirt, claw at his chest, beg him not to go. But she didn't and wouldn't.

Moments later, she heard the front door shut. The house was wrapped in a blanket of silence.

Victoria proceeded down the hallway and found the conference room. The door was slightly open. She saw Phillip through the crack in the door. He smiled.

"Excuse me, gentlemen." He got up from the table and went to the door, closing it behind him. "Hey, baby." He smiled broadly and kissed her. "What a surprise."

"More than you can imagine. I just wanted you to know that I just slapped some sense into your assistant and I'm going home now to prepare for my family's visit."

Phillip blinked rapidly. "You did what?"

"I just slapped your assistant. And you know what, it felt damned good."

"Victoria." He took her by the arm and ushered her down the hall. "What in the world happened?"

Victoria took a breath and spilled out the details that had unfolded outside his office door. As she spoke Phillip's face grew red with outrage and his midnight-blue eyes flashed. By the time she'd finished, he could barely contain his anger. He snatched her by the hand and marched off to his office.

Caitlyn was on the phone when he approached. He grabbed the phone out of her hand and tossed it across the desk. Her mouth opened in protest, but not a word came out.

"You have about five minutes to pack your stuff and get the hell out. Now."

Caitlyn stood, her large breasts heaving as she spoke. She pointed an accusing finger at Victoria. "She struck me!"

"And if I wasn't a man who was raised not to hit women I would hit you myself. Now get out."

Caitlyn's face went crimson. She sputtered and stuttered to no avail.

"When you mess with my wife you mess with me. Not only did you read personal information, you tried to use it against the woman I love, the mother of my child. You're despicable and if you don't move any faster, I'll let her smack you again—for me."

It took all Victoria had not to bust out in laughter. She would have paid good money to see this scene unfold. *You go, Phillip,* she thought, holding tight to his hand.

Caitlyn snatched up her purse and grabbed her suit jacket from the back of her chair.

"And don't even think about pressing charges," he said. "I'll sue you for slander and breach of confidence. You'll never work again."

Caitlyn huffed as tears streamed down her face. She flashed Victoria one last look and ran down the hallway.

Phillip reached for the phone and dialed security.

"Yes, this is Phillip Hunter. We have a disgruntled employee who has just been terminated by me. Caitlyn Singleton. She's on her way out. Be sure she finds her way to the curb."

Phillip hung up and turned to Victoria. Concern lit his eyes. "Are you okay?"

Victoria actually giggled. "Never been better." She angled her head to the side. "So this is what it's like to be 'round-the-way folks.'"

Phillip chuckled and put his arm around her waist. "I like it!"

They both laughed.

"I think I've worked up an appetite," Victoria quipped.

"Then by all means, let me take my beautiful, no-nonsense wife out to lunch."

Hours later, Toni wandered downstairs suddenly famished. Her intention was to fix something quick and easy, return to her bed, and watch a movie. But she stopped in her tracks when she reached the kitchen and saw what was on the table.

Torn in four large pieces were the papers she'd just signed, with a short note next to them. With a shaky hand she picked up the note with Charles's familiar handwriting. *The thought of my life without you in it is not possible. I'll be back later—for good. We'll talk.*

Toni held the note to her chest and squeezed her eyes shut.

Chapter 32

The phone rang and Regina picked it up in the living room.

"Hello?"

"Hey, babe, it's me."

Regina smiled. "Well, I sure hope it is. What's up?" She tugged on the drawstring of her sweatpants, ready to go to the gym.

"I'm downstairs. I want you to take a ride with me. We still have some unfinished business."

She took the cordless phone, went to the window, and looked out onto the street below.

"Unfinished business?"

"Yeah. You dressed?"

"Not for a night out on the town, but I'm decent. I was going to the gym."

"Fine. Come on down. I'll drop you off when we're done."

"What is this about, Parker?"

"You ask too many questions. Just grab your things and come down."

She exhaled a breath. "Okay. Give me a minute." She hung up and wondered what Parker had up his sleeve.

"That was five minutes," he teased when she opened the door and got in.

"A woman's prerogative. Now are you going to tell me what this is about?"

"I figure if we're going to really play out this thing between us, we need to get rid of all the old baggage and settle any old issues."

She angled herself in the seat. "Parker Heywood, what in the world are you talking about?"

"You'll see. Just relax." He pulled off and headed to downtown Brooklyn.

"How is Tracy?" she asked.

"Not good but better. At least she's talking a little more. She's eating and sleeping better."

"That's good. I haven't had a chance to talk with Toni, but maybe she can recommend someone. As a matter of fact I need to go by and see her. I know she's home, but all I get is her answering machine for the past few days. Kinda worried about her."

"You want to swing by there later?"

"Hmmm. Yes. That's more important than the gym. I'd never forgive myself if something happened and I hadn't been paying attention." She was pensive for a moment. "You have to really be desperate to want to take your own life," she said.

"And you never know what it will be to push that button."

"True."

Regina sat back and relaxed to the music, resigning herself to the fact that Parker wasn't going to give up any information.

As they approached the shopping center, Regina

realized that they were slowing down near the lingerie shop. She snapped her head in his direction. "Where are we going?"

"We're going to settle some unfinished business once and for all. I don't want you to have any lingering doubts about me or us." He cruised to a parking space and stopped. "Come on. I want you right there with me." He got out of the car and put a quarter in the meter for fifteen minutes. "That's more than enough time." He took Regina's hand and walked toward the store.

Victoria paced and rechecked every crack and crevice of the house. She looked at her watch, then went upstairs and checked her appearance in the mirror. She went back down and turned off the oven, opened the fridge to make sure that the wine was chilling and that the salad had not wilted. She wanted everything to be perfect.

Her baby was doing a little dance in her stomach.

"I'm scared, too," she said, rubbing her belly.

When she heard the key turn in the lock she nearly jumped out of her skin. She tugged in a shuddering breath and forced one foot in front of the other until she reached the foyer.

The door opened and Phillip stood there with a gentle, loving smile on his face. He opened the door wider to let the guests enter.

Victoria gasped and covered her mouth with her hand. In front of her was the perfect image of herself, from the slope of her eyes to the rise of her cheeks, the lift of her lips, the crystal-clear ebony complexion. It was like looking in a mirror a dozen years into the future.

The woman slowly approached, her eyes filled with wonder and sparkling with sudden tears.

"Victoria," she whispered, the name almost sounding like a prayer. The voice Victoria had heard in her dreams.

Victoria couldn't move. She dared not or the wonderful dream might vanish before her eyes.

Phillip took Ellen's hand and walked with her to Victoria.

"Baby, this is your mother, Ellen Lawry."

Ellen gazed upon her long-lost daughter with awe. "I prayed every day of my life that I would find you one day," she said. She raised a smooth, unwrinkled hand and touched Victoria's cheek as if she could not believe she was real.

Victoria's eyes drifted closed at the gentle touch and she clasped her own hand atop her mother's to hold it in place, to absorb the warmth and love that flowed from her fingertips.

Tears ran unbidden from beneath her closed lids. "Mama," she whispered.

"Ready?" Parker asked with his hand on the door of Brown Sugar.

"As ready as you are."

Parker pulled the door open and they stepped inside. They both spotted Kelly at the same time on the far side of the store talking to a customer.

Kelly turned with a ready smile on her face that froze in place when she saw who stood at the door.

Parker took Regina's hand and walked up to the counter.

"Excuse me," she murmured to her customer. With trepidation she approached the couple. She jutted her chin defiantly. "I don't know what lie he's—"

"Don't even go there, Kelly. It's not me that's lying, it's you. I told Regina everything: how we met, what went on, and even the night I came to your apartment—and how I left *without* sleeping with you."

For a moment she was stumped but she quickly recovered. "You're lying. We did sleep together, and I'm pregnant—with your baby."

"Fine. We'll go with you to a clinic first thing in the morning for a test," he challenged.

Kelly breathed heavily. Her throat worked up and down. She turned cold eyes on Regina. "I deal with women like you every day, women who have it all and think that I'm nothing but a salesgirl." She laughed. "That's what you thought, too, Parker. You thought you could sleep with me whenever you wanted and it would be okay. But it wasn't okay."

Parker looked at her with sad eyes. "I never lied to you, Kelly. Maybe I was wrong for getting involved with you the way I did, thinking that there was no responsibility for it on my part. But I never lied to you. I never told you that it was more than what it was or that it ever could be more. And you know that."

She folded her arms and lowered her head. "Just go."

"Kelly, I know I may be the last person you want to hear anything from," Regina said. "But people will do to you only what you allow them to do and for as long as you allow it. Believe me, I know from experience."

Kelly slowly raised her head and saw the sincerity in Regina's eyes. She turned and walked away.

Parker tugged in a deep breath and put his arm around Regina's shoulder. "Come on, let's go see Toni."

Victoria's newfound family sat around her living room following the early meal she'd prepared. Her sister, Felicia, was the spitting image of their father, she noted as her sister got up to chase after little Victoria, who decided to investigate upstairs.

"You're every bit as wonderful as I imagined," her dad said.

Phillip draped his arm around his wife. "She's quite spectacular."

"And I'm going to have another grandbaby," her mother said, delight shining in her smile.

Victoria giggled. "I think it's a football player," she said, gently massaging an elbow that was poking her in the ribs.

"We need some more men in the family," her father intoned. "I've been getting the devil for years."

Ellen gave him a playful slap on the thigh. "And he loves every minute of it. Little Vikki has him wrapped around her finger."

"I bet she does," Phillip said. "And son or daughter, I know I'm going to spoil them rotten." He hugged Victoria.

As Victoria relaxed within the embrace of her husband, enjoying the love and laughter of her family, she knew without question that this was what she had been searching for all of her life. She understood that after the first blush of excitement had passed, they had a lot of talking to do. The lost years could never be recovered but they had a whole future to look forward to. She glanced at her mother, who was rocking her niece on her lap, and she hoped that she looked just like her mother in the years to come.

"That was eye-opening," Parker said as he got onto the Brooklyn Bridge en route to Manhattan and Toni's house.

"We never know how our actions are going to affect other people," Regina said. "We just go through life doing our thing, sometimes oblivious of the outcome until it hits you in the face."

"Yeah, you're right. I'm just sorry that you had to go through that."

"It's settled now. I just hope Kelly will be okay."

"Yeah, me too."

They pulled up in front of Toni's brownstone and Regina was relieved to see lights on in the upstairs bedroom.

"Looks like she's home," she said.

"Want me to come in with you?"

"No. This will only take a minute. I just want to make sure she's okay." She unfastened her seat belt and got out.

She walked to the front door and rang the bell, remembering all too vividly the last time she was there.

Moments later, Toni answered the door, looking radiant and dressed in nothing more than a Victoria's Secret robe.

"Hey, G. What are you doing here?" She smiled brightly and tugged on the sash of her robe.

"Uh, I just dropped by to check on you and—"

"Who's at the door, sugah?"

Toni looked over her shoulder, and Regina caught

a glimpse of Charles in the background in a pair of boxers and nothing else.

"It's Regina," Toni called out.

Charles waved. "Hey, Gina. I'll be upstairs waiting for you, T," he said and disappeared up the staircase.

Toni turned back to Regina and grinned mischievously. She shrugged. "We're, uh, working things out."

Regina's eyes widened in amusement. "Working things out or working out?"

Toni giggled. "A little of both."

Regina's expression grew serious. "Are you sure this time, Toni?"

Toni sighed deeply. "Can any of us be sure of anything?" she asked. "All I can do is give it my best shot."

Regina leaned forward and kissed the cheek of her friend. "Just be happy," she said.

"Yeah," Toni said. "That's what I'm aiming for."

Regina turned to leave. "And don't hurt yourself in the process, sis." She gave Toni a wink and sprinted back to the car.

"Everything okay?" Parker asked.

Regina turned to him. "Yeah, I think so," she said, a soft smile framing her mouth. "I think so."

Parker glanced at her quizzically but didn't press the issue. "Where to?"

"You know what I was thinking?" She chewed on her thumbnail.

"Should I really answer that?"

She playfully rolled her eyes. "I was thinking that I would fix dinner tonight at my place and that you could bring Tracy."

"You sure you want to do that?"

"Absolutely. I'm sure she would like getting out of the house, and there's no time like the present for her to meet Michele and Darren."

Parker nodded. "Okay. We'll be there."

"Good."

Regina sat back, thinking about the swinging turn of events. Today was certainly a day for revelations and moving on. And if she intended to move on with Parker, there were still loose ends that she needed to tie up as well.

Chapter 33

Regina watched from the window until Parker's car was out of sight. She took out a whole chicken that she had been defrosting in the refrigerator, fresh broccoli from the bin, and a bag of wild rice from the overhead cabinet. She quickly washed and seasoned the chicken and placed it in a roasting pan and covered it with aluminum foil. She cut up the broccoli, seasoned it and placed it in a pot on the stove, and covered it. She took a brief look around, satisfied that she had everything she needed.

"Michele! Darren!"

"Yes," they replied in harmony.

"Come here a minute."

Shortly, they filed into the kitchen with identical looks of "I didn't do anything" on their faces.

"Have a seat."

They pulled out chairs from beneath the kitchen table and sat down.

Regina took a breath. "I'm having company for

dinner tonight. Parker and his daughter, Tracy, are coming."

Michele and Darren stole glances at each other, then at their mother.

"Tracy could really use some friends right now."

"Why?" Darren asked in his always direct way.

Regina sat down. "She just lost her mother. Parker brought her here from California to live with him. So she's hurting right now and doesn't have any friends. I want you two to be nice to her and show her around."

"How old is she?" Michele asked.

"Fifteen."

"What happened to her mother?" Darren wanted to know.

"She was . . . sick."

"With what?" he probed.

"I don't really know," she lied. They didn't need to know, at least not now.

Michele folded her arms. "She's kinda young to hang out with me," she said.

"I didn't say you had to be joined at the hip, but you can show her around."

"Hmm. Okay," she agreed reluctantly.

"What's she look like?" Darren said, realizing that fifteen was right up his alley.

Regina held back a chuckle. "I don't know. I'll be meeting her for the first time tonight myself."

"Is that it?" Michele asked.

"Yes. I need to run out for about an hour. I'm putting the chicken in the oven before I leave. Just keep an eye on it for me until I get back."

"Okay."

Regina got up from the table. "Thanks, guys."

They mumbled something and hustled back to their rooms.

Regina put the chicken in the oven, then darted off to her own room and got out of her sweats. She put on a pair of jeans and a white blouse. She looked at the phone, debating whether she should call first, and decided that she should. She knew how put out she always felt when unexpected visitors turned up on her doorstep.

She picked up the phone and punched in the numbers.

"Hey, honey," Parker said, finding Tracy in the bedroom. "Sorry it took me so long." He walked in and sat in a chair opposite the bed. "How ya doing?"

Tracy shrugged. "Okay, I guess."

"Listen, I have a surprise for you."

"What?"

"We were invited out to dinner."

She cut her eyes in his direction. "Where?"

"Remember when I told you about my friend Regina?"

She didn't respond.

"Well, she invited us to her house for dinner. She wants to meet you and she wants you to meet her daughter and son."

"I don't feel like going. Why can't we order something and stay here?"

"Tracy, you've been cooped up in this house since you got here. That's not cool. I think getting out for a few hours will be good for you."

Tracy folded her arms and pouted. "What if they don't like me, like everybody else?"

Parker frowned as the topic of Tracy's friend-lessness rose again. "Baby, why do you say that?"

She turned her dark green eyes on him. " 'Cause nobody does," she said in a thready voice.

"Why? You're a wonderful girl."

"How would you know?" she snapped.

"Tracy, come on, I'm not the enemy."

She twisted her lips.

"Tell me why you feel that way."

She glanced down. "All the black kids in school always teased me about my hair, my complexion. Said I thought I was white. And the white kids didn't want to be bothered 'cause they know I'm black."

Parker's heart felt as if it just broke in two. He got up from the chair and came to sit next to her.

"Look at me, Tracy."

Reluctantly, she glanced up.

"You are a beautiful, intelligent young lady, one brought into this world by two people who loved each other against the odds. And all those silly, bigoted fools were only reacting out of ignorance and jealousy. Them not taking you into their lives is their loss, not yours, sweetheart. Life is ugly, people are ugly, but we can't let either beat us down."

"You don't know what it's like not to fit in," she said, her eyes filling.

"No, you're right, I don't know. Just like you don't know how hard it is to be a black man in America. We both got a raw deal. But we can't let that beat us, 'cause we are better than that." He paused. "I can't promise that things are going to be perfect with you living here in New York. But I can promise that when all else fails I'll be the best friend you ever had." He brushed her silky soft hair and she pressed her head against his chest.

Parker held her and wished that he had the power to make life smooth sailing for her. But all he could do was his best. So this was parenthood, he thought as he held his daughter close. He still had so much to learn.

Regina pulled up in front of the apartment building and got out. As she rode the elevator to the sixth floor, she tried to go over in her head everything she had to say. She'd been down this road once before, but foolishly she'd left the door open for the past to walk back in. It wasn't right and it wasn't fair to either of them.

She walked up to 6C and knocked on the door.

Moments later, Russell appeared.

"It must be important to bring you to my door. Come on in."

Regina stepped inside. She'd never been to Russell's place since they'd been divorced. She was pleasantly surprised by his taste in furniture and the neatness of it all. Russell had never been much of a homemaker. She'd done pretty much everything when it came to taking care of the house and kids. He felt his only role was to make the money to pay the bills, and the rest was up to her.

"Nice place," she said, turning to face him.

"Thanks. Have a seat." He extended his hand toward the couch. "Can I get you anything?"

"No. I'm not staying."

He looked at her for moment. He slid his hands in his pockets. "So . . . what's on your mind, Regina?"

"Us."

"Hmm. I see." He sat on the love seat opposite her. "I'm listening."

"Russell . . . I will always care about you. You were my very first. But I'm not in love with you any longer. I tried to fool myself into believing that something could still be happening between us . . . that night. It can't, Russ. I'm in love with Parker, really *in* love with him. And we need a fair shot if we're going to make it work."

"So all these weeks, all the things I've said, the years we spent together, none of that means anything. Is that what you're telling me?"

"It all meant something, Russ, just not what you want it to. What we had was between two different people. I'm not the same woman and you're not the same man. This is not like a childhood game that we can do over. We can't and I think you know that."

He breathed a short chuckle through his nose. "I guess I've known that all along. But you can't blame a brother for trying." He forced a smile. "So does this mean I can't flirt with you either?" he asked, his dark eyes dancing with mischief.

"Flirting is always good for a woman's ego, but in our case I think that would pose a real problem."

He twisted his lips. "I don't know how to just be your friend, Gina."

"I don't know how to be yours either. Guess that's something we'll have to work on, for our sakes and the kids."

He nodded slowly, then looked at her. "You're really something," he said, admiration evident in his tone. "I wonder if that dude . . ."

"You mean Parker?" she tossed out.

"Yeah, yeah, Parker. I wonder if he knows how lucky he is."

She grinned. "I think he has a pretty good idea." She stood up and inhaled a cleansing breath.

Russell got up and walked her to the door. "I'll make sure I call before I come from now on."

"I'd appreciate that." She put her hand on the door.

"Gina."

She turned and looked up at him.

He touched her cheek with the tip of his finger as he let his gaze run lazily across her face. "I'll always love ya, G."

She cupped his face in her hands and brought her lips to his to touch lightly for the very last time, then turned and walked out feeling more free and clear in her conscience than she had in a very long time.

As she drove back home she realized why she'd been unable to fully commit to Parker, to allow him totally into her spirit. There'd been no room because she was still clinging to the past. A past that could never be recovered.

There would always be a place for Russell in her heart. She knew she'd thought and said it all before. But this time she'd been faced with a challenge she'd never previously confronted. Life and death. She chose to take her chances on life with Parker. And the moment she made that decision she knew what true love really was.

When she returned home, the chicken was done and sitting covered on the top of the stove. The broccoli was cooked and the rice was finished. When she walked into the small dining room, she was stopped in her tracks.

The table was set with her best china, linen napkins, and her good glasses. And in the center of the table was a vase of fresh red roses. She placed her hands on her hips and shook her head. Wonders never ceased.

She turned and Michele was standing in the doorway.

"I thought it would be kind of nice to have flowers," she said.

"A very nice and thoughtful touch, Michele. Thank you."

Michele lowered her head and stepped in. "Ma, I kinda thought about what you said after you left. I mean about Parker's daughter losing her mother and everything."

"Yes . . ."

Michele shrugged her right shoulder. "And I started thinking about how I would feel if . . . I lost you." She looked at her mother.

"Oh, Shell." Regina held out her arms and her daughter walked into them. "I plan on being here for a very long time," she said against Michele's hair. "Who's going to give you a hard time otherwise?"

Michele laughed and sniffed. "I better change clothes. What time are they coming?"

"They should be here around eight." Regina patted Michele's back. "Go on and change and I think I will, too."

Regina watched as her daughter left the room and hoped that she would not break the promise she made to her.

* * *

Later that evening, Regina and Parker sat out on the front steps while the kids watched a movie after dinner.

Parker put his arm around Regina's shoulder. "Well, we got past the first hurdle," he said.

"Tracy is a lovely girl."

"Thanks. And I really appreciate your kids hanging out with her. It's good for her." He paused a moment. "Something she said to me today really rocked me."

Regina turned to look at him. "What?"

Parker told her what Tracy said about the kids in school.

"Oh, the poor baby." She sighed deeply. "Kids can be so cruel. Funny, Victoria went through the same thing, still going through it, but on the opposite end of the spectrum."

"Hmph, and to look at her you'd never really think anything got to Victoria."

"I know. Her color is her Achilles' heel." She lowered her voice. "I never knew Lynn was white."

"I never thought it was important." He turned to her. "Does it matter? That I was married to a white woman?"

"No. Just interesting, that's all."

"Interesting like how?"

"Hmm, I always wondered what attracted black men to white women and if the whole myth of forbidden fruit was behind it."

Parker chuckled. "I wish it was as mystical as all that. Simple truth was we liked each other. We had the same interests, same likes." He shrugged. "Like any couple."

Regina nodded. "Tracy is going to need some-one in her life, a woman friend."

"I know. I'm hoping that you'll try to step in . . . when you can."

"I'd love to. I was already telling Michele that maybe the three of us could go shopping or some-thing and maybe Tracy can help out in the store until she goes back to school. Have you looked into that?"

"Next on my agenda. I'm still waiting for her records to be sent to me."

"She could probably get into school with Michele and Darren. At least she would have some familiar faces."

"Sounds good. As soon as her records come I'll take her down. There's only a couple more months left and I know the transition is going to be rough."

Regina rested her head on Parker's shoulder. "I think Tracy is going to be just fine."

"What about us? How are we?"

"I think we'll be okay, too. We have a lot of work ahead of us."

"And a lot of adjustments. How are we going to be together? I can't stay here and you can't stay at my place anymore."

"I know."

He clasped her chin and lifted her face to look into his eyes. "It's killing me being away from you," he said softly. "I certainly can't wait until the kids grow up and move out."

Regina grinned. "So what do you suggest?"

"We need to plan some away time. Me and you. I'll make love to you day and night and wait on you hand and foot."

"Hmmm, sounds lovely."

"Or you could just marry me and make me an honest man."

Regina's heart stuttered in her chest.

"Yeah, you heard me right, Regina Everette. I want to marry you. I want you to be my wife. I want to spend the rest of my life loving you, taking care of you and these kids. But . . . I want to prove to you that I'm the man you need to spend the rest of your life with. And when you're sure . . . absolutely without a doubt sure . . . then say yes."

She started to speak, but he covered her mouth in a mind-numbing kiss.

Tracy watched it all from the top of the stairs in the doorway. She'd just lost her mother and now she was going to lose her father too. She spun away and ran back up the stairs.

Chapter 34

Parker knocked on Tracy's bedroom door.

"Trace. Are you just about ready?"

She snatched open the door, still in her pajamas. Parker frowned.

"Why aren't you dressed? It's time to go. I told Regina we'd meet her at the store at two."

"I don't want to go."

"Why, Tracy?" he asked, trying to contain his exasperation. This back and forth had been going on with Tracy for the past two weeks. Any time he mentioned getting together with Regina, Tracy was suddenly ill or too tired. He'd run out of reasons to tell Regina why he couldn't see her. Of course she said she understood. But how long could this go on? He had to steal time between classes to run down to the store and see her for an hour. He felt like a teenager on curfew and it was beginning to mess with his head.

"I don't want to go."

"I'll ask you again. Why?"

"Why can't we spend the day together, just you and me?"

"Tracy, that's all we've been doing, sweetie. You've been with me to my classes. We've had dinner together every night, watched movies together. You've sat here with me while I worked."

"So why can't we keep doing that?"

"Tracy . . . listen to me." He braced her shoulders and looked down into her eyes. "I know this time is really hard. I know you're scared to get out in the world. But you'll never get past that fear if you don't try. And I'm going to be truthful with you. I miss Regina. She's important to me and I want to spend time with her. Can you understand that?"

"I heard you that night on the steps at *her* house. You're going to leave me just like Mommy did!"

Parker was taken aback by her vehemence. "Tracy. I'm not going to leave you. I—"

"Yes, you are. You're going to leave me for her! She's gonna be more important than me, just like . . . just like . . ."

"Just like what, baby, just like what?"

"Just like Paul was to Mommy. All they wanted to do was be with each other. They never paid me any attention. I didn't have anyone." She was crying outright now.

"Oh God, baby." He took her in his arms and held her, wishing he could squeeze out all the hurt and loneliness that had filled her life. He was more tortured than ever before for all the years that he missed, that he might have been able to make a difference had he been given the chance. "Shhh, it's okay. It's okay. I'm not going to leave you. Listen, let's make a deal."

Tracy sniffed hard and wiped at her eyes. "What?"

"We go out today. Hang with Regina, and then tomorrow you and I will hang out. Just us. Deal?" He looked at her with hopeful eyes.

Tracy made a face. "Okay," she murmured.

Parker released a sigh of relief. "Great. You want to go and get dressed now? If you put a little pep in your step we'll only be a half hour late."

While Tracy got ready Parker went to the phone in the studio and called Regina at the store.

"Hang on a second, Mr. Heywood. She's in the back," Renee said.

Regina came to the phone a few minutes later.

"Don't tell me, you're not coming," she said instead of hello.

"Actually, I was calling to say that we were coming, but running late."

"Everything okay?"

"Yes and no. I'll talk to you about it a little later. Michele and Darren there?"

"Michele came about an hour ago. Darren opted to go with his friends to a basketball game."

"We'll be there soon."

"See you then," she said and hung up the phone. She stood there for a moment with her hand still on the receiver. She didn't know if it was funny or scary that she was getting accustomed to Parker breaking their dates lately.

Fortunately she had enough to keep her busy and her mind occupied. Between the store and her own family, she'd taken an evening off to visit Victoria's family before they returned to Atlanta.

She couldn't believe how Victoria had bloomed and she didn't mean from the pregnancy. There was a glow about her, an inner certainty that radiated in everything she did, from the way she walked and spoke to the way she looked at her husband and talked about her any-minute-now pregnancy with actual joy. There was a confidence there that was no longer superficial but one that Victoria truly felt inside. She'd finally found that person she'd been searching for—herself.

As for Toni, she'd taken a leave of absence from work and was playing the role of wife and mother. She loved it, she'd confided, but knew she'd have to get back out into the real world soon. She and Charles were going to counseling and it looked as if they were really going to make it.

They all promised to have dinner at their old hangout, the Shark Bar, before Victoria had the baby. They had a lot of catching up to do and Regina had plenty to tell her friends.

Plenty wasn't the half of it. Since everything had unfolded with Kelly, then the HIV scare, her almost romp with Russell, and now trying to figure out how to make things work with her and Parker and the kids, especially Tracy, she'd been on a roller-coaster ride of emotion. And no one to spill her guts to. It would be good to get together with her girls. Maybe they might be able to lend some advice on how she should handle the delicate situation with Tracy.

It was apparent that Tracy had a real problem with her and her father being together. Regina knew that Tracy was still grieving for her mother, and that was understandable. But all she wanted to do was have a chance to get to know her. If she and Parker were to stand any chance of being together on a permanent basis, *Tracy* was going to have to find a way to allow Regina into her life.

Regina moved away from the desk and headed to the back of the store. And *she* was going to have to find a way to win Tracy's heart and her trust.

Parker, Tracy, Regina, and Michele piled into Parker's car and they headed off to Manhattan. Regina figured that after doing some window- and some real shopping, there were plenty of restaurants to choose from for dinner and the atmosphere of Manhattan was always great.

"What kinds of clothes do you like?" Regina asked from the backseat.

Tracy shrugged. "Whatever. It doesn't matter."

Michele snatched a look at her mother but held her tongue.

"What do you think, Michele, should we go to the Village?" Regina asked, hoping to fill the conversation gap.

"I love the Village and you know I know every store."

"Yes, my pocket knows very well." Regina leaned forward and put her hand on Parker's shoulder. Tracy moved closer to her father. Regina frowned. "Parker, let's go to the Village and then we can go uptown."

"Not a problem."

Regina eased back into her seat and assessed

the scene in front of her. This was going to be a
very long day.

And things only got worse. Whatever Regina
suggested, Tracy didn't want any part of. If Regina
tried to talk to Parker or get near him, Tracy found
something that she had to tell him or found a way
to ease herself between them. When they walked
down the street, it was Tracy who held Parker's hand
and sat next to him in the restaurant.

By the time Parker dropped Regina and Michele
off at her house, Regina was emotionally drained.
She couldn't get out of the car fast enough.

"I hope you had a good time today, Tracy," Regina
said, before getting out.

"It was okay."

Michele rolled her eyes. "See ya, Parker. Bye,
Tracy," she said and got out.

"Good night," Regina said and got out behind
Michele.

"I'll be right back," Parker said to Tracy and
made a move to get out.

"But I'm tired. I want to go home."

He snapped his head in her direction and pointed
a finger at her. "You wait here until I get back,
whether it's five minutes or five hours." He got out
of the car. "Regina, wait."

She stopped. Her shoulders slumped and she
turned around. "How is this ever going to work?" she
asked, shaking her head as he approached. "Tracy
has no intention of letting anyone in your life except
her. That's pretty obvious." She took a breath. "And I
can understand it, especially with what she's been
through and from all that you've told me. I just don't
know how long I can deal with it."

Parker stepped up to her and held her by the shoulders. "I know this is hard. It's hard for me too. I just need you to hang in there with me a little longer. She starts school next week and I've been looking for a counselor for her. I know that will help."

Regina nodded her head. "I'm the last one who should gripe about troublesome kids. Mine weren't pillars of society either for a while."

"How well I remember." He laughed lightly. "So can you hang in there with me?" He stepped a little closer.

She felt the warmth of his body surround her, and the feel of his fingertips at the back of her neck nearly had her moaning out loud in the middle of the street. She knew part of her frustration was pure sexual deprivation, plain and simple. She missed being with Parker physically. She missed his touch. She missed feeling him fill her. She missed the intimate moments that they shared after they made love. *Grrrr, kids,* she thought.

She reached up and stroked his cheek. "I can hang on if you can."

"That's why I love ya." He leaned down and kissed her. "I'll call you tomorrow."

"I might just have to rearrange my back office for an afternoon tryst." Her eyes darkened with want.

"I'll bring the sandwiches." He winked and headed back to the car.

Regina went upstairs. Making love in her office. Just the idea excited her. She could lock the door, turn on some music and . . . Hmmm, the way she was feeling, that scenario was looking better by the minute. She knew that futon she'd stashed in there would come in handy one day.

She crawled under the covers that night with a smile on her face.

Chapter 35

Regina arrived at the bookstore super early. She wanted to be sure she beat Renee in. She didn't need to have her assistant actually seeing what she was up to. She came into the store and locked it behind her and went straight to the back with her packages.

She took a quick inventory of the space and started making some necessary adjustments. She moved the worktable from the center of the room against the far wall. She took out the bottle of wine and put it in the mini refrigerator. Then she took out the towels and washcloths that she'd brought from home and put them in the tiny bathroom.

From her shopping bag of tricks she pulled out a set of sheets and opened the futon to put them on. Her mini stereo was always set to the jazz station, so she turned it on and lowered the volume to a cozy level.

Regina took a breath and looked at her handi-work. She grinned. She should have thought of this weeks ago. The only thing missing now was the man of the hour. He promised to bring lunch, but she doubted very seriously if they would get a chance to eat—at least not any food, she thought wickedly.

Satisfied that there was nothing more to be done until Parker arrived, she closed up the room and went out front to get started with her day.

The hours seemed to crawl by. When Regina looked at the clock it was eleven. When she looked again at what seemed like an hour later, it was eleven-fifteen.

"Are you okay, Ms. Everette?" Renee asked. "You seem totally distracted."

"Just a few things on my mind," she said and snuck a look at the clock again. Parker promised to be there by noon. He took Tracy to school for her first day, and he had a class at three and needed to be on his way by two-thirty. That gave them at least two hours, Regina thought greedily. The way she was feeling she wasn't sure if even that was enough time.

When the bell over the door chimed and she saw Parker walking through the door, looking good enough to serve up on a platter, she nearly squealed out loud.

He had that dangerously hungry look in his eyes, and the way his locks moved around his face when he walked gave him a mysteriously exotic look, one of the first things that had attracted her to him.

She swallowed over the sudden dryness in her throat and struggled to keep from snatching him by the hand and dragging him to the back room.

"Hi," he said as he eased up to the counter where Regina stood.

"Hi yourself." She looked down at the bag in his hand. "Whatcha got?"

"Treats."

"Hey, Mr. Heywood," Renee said, walking up on the couple, oblivious of the sparks popping between them.

"Hi, Renee. How are you?"

"Great. I sold another one of your pieces this morning," she said proudly.

"I think I need to hire you as my personal salesperson." He grinned. "You're going to singlehandedly make me famous. How's school?"

"All done except for finals."

"Well, good luck with them."

"Thanks. Ms. Everette, I was going to take my lunch break. I need to run a couple of errands. Is that okay?"

Panic and disappointment seized Regina's heart and squeezed. No, she silently screamed. She would not be denied. Not today, not again. *Think, Regina.*

"Uh . . . sure. As a matter of fact, why don't you take off the rest of the day? Mondays are always slow. I can handle it."

Renee frowned slightly. "Are you sure?"

"Positive. It will be fine."

"Okay. Take care, Mr. Parker."

"You too, Renee."

She got her purse from behind the counter. "If things get too hectic just call me on my cell phone and I can come back."

"I'm sure I won't need to but I'll keep it in mind."

Regina waited until Renee was gone and hustled over to the front door. She put up the closed sign and locked the door. Slowly she turned toward Parker, a smile of invitation on her lips.

"Come into my parlor, said the spider to the fly," she said.

"I'd get trapped in your web any day."

"I was hoping you'd say that." Regina took his hand and led him to the back room.

The instant they were behind closed doors they were like two lost travelers who'd been wandering the desert and finally found an oasis. Every touch, every kiss, every moan and sigh was amplified. Eager hands and hungry mouths sought out all the hidden places and the room itself seemed to vibrate with their heat.

"I missed you," Parker groaned against her mouth as he slid his hand under her T-shirt and unsnapped her bra.

"You're going to have to show me just how much until I tell you to stop," she said, unbuckling his belt.

"Hmmm. You know how much I love a challenge." He eased her back toward the futon and they both collapsed on top of it. Parker looked down into her honey-brown eyes as she lay beneath him. "And you know how much I love you."

He started at her neck, planting tiny hot kisses along her collarbone. He pushed her shirt up and over her head, tossing it to the floor.

"These . . . these are always so exquisite," he murmured as he paid due homage to her breasts, licking, nipping, caressing until she cried out for more.

Parker smiled. He eased down to her stomach and let his tongue play in the hollow of her navel while he slid her slacks and panties down over her hips. He inhaled her scent and it sent of jolt of electricity right to his penis, making it throb with longing.

He placed tender kisses in the soft down, savoring the moment when he could taste the very essence of her. Regina moaned when he cupped her hips and raised them to meet his mouth and exploring tongue.

Regina cried out his name and gripped the sheet in her fists when his tongue ran hot circles around her clit. Her entire body trembled as if it had no will of its own and she rotated her pelvis in rhythm to the flicks of Parker's tongue and lips to heighten the pleasure he was evoking in her.

Her first climax hit her like a speeding train, roaring through her with such force that it took her breath away and paralyzed her limbs. And then she shook uncontrollably as she succumbed to the second one. She whimpered, "Enough."

"I'm not finished yet," Parker said, his voice hot and thick. He took a condom out of his pants pocket.

Regina struggled to sit up. "Let me do it," she whispered.

He handed her the condom and got on his knees. She took his rock-hard sex in one hand and the condom in the other, placing it over the tip. By torturing degrees she slowly rolled it down the length of him, massaging him as she went along.

"You're very good," he said and kissed her. "Very good." He eased her back down on the bed and worked his way in between her thighs—spreading them. "This is what I've been dreaming about." He raised her right leg and then her left, bracing her thighs wide open with his shoulders. He pushed closer, rising up on his knees until he felt the heat of her vagina calling out to him.

When he felt himself slide into her heat his head actually spun and he gripped the wall in front of him to keep from falling.

"Oh, yesss," he hissed through his teeth, then grabbed her hips in both hands and stroked her long and deep.

"So good, so good," she whimpered, working her insides to open and contract around every move he made inside her. She gripped his back and her eyes opened wide when she felt another orgasm ready to seize her. And she knew it would be even more intense than the others.

It began at the bottom of her feet, and continued up her legs, rippling up her back along her spine, wrapping itself around her and hardening her nipples, then rushing down to her belly, making it quiver and dance. Sweat popped out along her hairline and the room suddenly felt as if it were consumed in fire. Her heart raced out of control as she felt Parker's erection grow even firmer. He was moaning her name, driving into her, and then all at once he gave an incredible shove and they both cried out as their bodies climaxed in unison, the indescribable sensation racing up and down their bodies.

It seemed to go on forever until their bodies simply jerked helplessly, and finally it subsided to a titillating throb and they lay spent and utterly satisfied.

Parker pulled Regina close. "We need to do this more often," he breathed in her ear. "Or else we might wind up killing each other."

Regina giggled. "I know. I don't remember it ever being like that."

"Me either."

"I love you, Gina."

"I love you, Parker."

"That's a good thing," he said. "A real good thing."

Michele hurried down the crowded hallway. She was finished with her classes for the day and couldn't wait to get out. She was supposed to meet some of her friends after school. As she turned out of one hallway and down another she ran smack into Tracy.

"Oh, man, I'm sorry," Michele said. "I didn't . . . Hey, Tracy."

"Hi." She held her books to her chest.

"First day?"

"Yeah."

"How is it so far?"

Tracy shrugged. "All right, I guess."

Michele tried not to get pissed off but Tracy was really getting on her last nerve. "Are you finished for today or do you have more classes?"

"I'm done."

"Good. Come on." She took Tracy by the arm and ushered her outside. When they got in the yard she turned to face her. "Look, I know you just lost your mom, and to be truthful I can't even imagine what that must be like. And I know it must be hard as hell—excuse my French—to get by day to day. So I can kind of understand how you act and everything, but what's not cool is how you treat my mom."

"I don't—"

"You know exactly what you do. You're rude, you're borderline nasty, and you act as though, if you turn your back, my mom is going to make your dad disappear right under your nose."

Tracy pursed her lips and held her books a little tighter to her chest.

"Look, I didn't like your dad too much when I first met him either. Gave him and my mom a natural fit." She shrugged. "I wanted my mother to get back together with my dad. But that's not going to happen and I'm pretty cool with it now. I realize that in order for me and my brother to be happy, my mom needs to be happy, and being with your dad makes her happy."

Tracy looked down at her shoes. "Your mom is okay. It's not that I don't like her. It's just that . . ."

"Hey, I know. I felt the same way." She gave Tracy a crooked smile. "Do you have to go right home?"

"Why?"

"I figured I'd introduce you to some of my friends. And if you want you can come over to my house and hang out for a while. You could call your dad and find out if it's okay."

Tracy smiled, really smiled. "Okay." She pulled out her cell phone and dialed her father's cell number.

Parker put his cell phone back down on the floor near the futon.

"Was that Tracy?" Regina asked.

"Yes, and you'll never guess what she asked me."

"What?"

"She asked if she could go with Michele to meet

some of her friends and wanted to know if I could pick her up from your house later."

Regina turned around on her side to face him, a smile of disbelief on her face. "Hey, maybe this relationship and family thing just might work after all."

"Yeah, maybe it will." He turned her onto her back and leaned above her. "And while it's working let's not deprive ourselves in the meantime." He lowered his head and kissed her.

"My sentiments exactly," she murmured against his lips.

Chapter 36

Regina emerged from the depths of the New York City subway system and walked the three blocks to Seventy-second Street. She opted to leave her car at home rather than fight Friday night traffic in Manhattan. She walked with an easy carefree stride, catching the eyes of many as she strutted along Broadway.

She felt pretty darn good, she had to admit. One hurdle after another had been thrown up in front of her in the past months and she'd been able to leap over every one of them. Sure she'd stumbled a few times, but she'd brushed herself off and kept going. That had to count for something.

Regina dipped her hands into the pockets of her flowing trench coat and wondered what the girls were going to run their mouths about tonight. They had so much catching up to do, but with the multitude of traumas running rampant in their lives, there just hadn't been time. She knew their eyes would be wide when she dropped her bombs on the table. She laughed to herself. It had ultimately wound up being her, the one least likely to cause a stir, who kept turning over the apple-cart.

The Shark Bar was up ahead. Regina pulled the door open and stepped inside.

As usual for a Friday night the joint was jumping. The bar was lined from one end to the next and every available table was filled. The tantalizing aroma of seafood, grilled beef, and down-home greens tempted the senses. The decimal level was at a bearable pitch with just enough background music to underscore the chorus of laughter and conversation.

Standing there in the doorway, Regina was taken back to one of the last times she'd been to the club with her girls. It was the day she'd quit her job and the day that signaled a new direction in their relationship as friends. She'd been pretty quiet the entire night, not sure how or when she was going to tell them. A part of her was so afraid of what their reactions might be that she'd pretty much tuned everything and everyone out of her head as she tried to figure out what she was going to say. It had been fast-talking Toni that cut into her preoccupation with her tongue-tied dilemma.

"Hmm. What's going on with you?" Toni had asked. *"You're in a strange place tonight."*

She remembered pulling in a lungful of air, and looking at them from beneath her lashes. There was that damned fluttering in her stomach again, she realized. "I quit my job today." She took a sip of water.

Victoria's perfectly made up face visibly dropped. Toni's celery stick slipped from her fingers with a tiny plop into the dressing.

"What did you say?" Toni babbled.

"I quit. Walked out. Handed in my resignation."

"So you have a better job somewhere else?" Victoria asked, certain that was the case.

"No. I don't."

"What! Gina, are you crazy? What in the world are you going to do?" Toni wailed.

"You know if you quit you don't get unemployment or anything," Victoria announced in a tone that sounded totally offended by the sheer stupidity of the situation.

"First, I'm not crazy. Second, I know what my options are."

"Fine. But you have two children to take care of," Toni insisted, certain that Regina had not factored them into her equation.

"I know I have two children," Regina responded in a flat monotone, struggling to keep a lid on her bubbling temper. "I know I have an apartment, a car and bills to pay for, and no health insurance." Her voice began to quake when she considered the sheer enormity of it all.

"How in the world are you going to manage, Regina? Michele will be ready for college in another year. Do you have a plan?" Victoria pressed.

"I will."

Toni and Victoria looked at each other in complete bewilderment.

Victoria leaned forward. "Listen, Gina, I'm sure the job had its downside, but if I recall correctly you were the one crying on our shoulders when you left Russell, wondering how you were going to make it. I told you then you needed to rethink things and stay with him. Nothing could *be that bad. And you two have kids together, for God's sake. Now look at you." She leaned back, her brows rising in a know-it-all attitude. "And whether you admit it or not, it was the biggest mistake you ever made. Now you're ready to make another one."*

"How could you just up and quit your only form of livelihood without a backup?" Toni cut in. "That's something a flighty teenager would do, not a grown woman with responsibilities. It wouldn't cross my mind: one, to leave my husband, and two, leave my job. Especially without something in the hole—another man and another job."

"You got that right. I worked too hard to get what I have, and I'll be damned if I'd just give it up on a whim," Victoria agreed. "Your mother is going to flip and I truly don't want to have to go through another scene with her like I did after your divorce," she continued as if this all were a personal attack on her.

"I think you're just going through an early midlife crisis thing, Gina," Toni stated with authority, emphasizing each point with her customary hand accompaniment. "You're going to be forty in a few weeks and it must be hitting you hard, throwing your hormones off. You know this happens to a lot of women, Gina," she ran on in her rapid-fire style. "I've treated so many women who have these . . . these false notions that turn their lives upside down and then they regret them. And, of course, they turn to me for help. Maybe you should go to counseling or something, get some of your inner problems dealt with by a professional. I could recommend someone. This is just so unlike you."

"Exactly. You're the one who's always been on the straight and narrow. Damn, what are the kids going to say? Have you thought about them at all? You know you

haven't been the same person since you left Russell."
Victoria shook her head sadly as if she were dealing with an irresponsible child.

They went on and on taking turns telling her how foolish she was, how irresponsible, how this was just another phase she was going through. Regina could feel the storm clouds building in her chest. She'd known these two women since college. They'd shared holidays, joys, sorrows, and too many a Friday night together. And she didn't know them. Neither did they know her. Maybe it was time to move away, not just from a job that was killing her spirit, but from people who couldn't care less about her as a person. People who only saw her as the good girl from next door, the one who would never do anything to upset anyone, people who totally underestimated her. It was painfully obvious that they took her behavior personally, that she was someone who needed fixing, not the situation. Just like when she finally left Russell. They couldn't believe that anything could be so terrible that she would give up her wonderful life.

Now this. Well, she couldn't sit back and take it anymore. She couldn't. If she did, she'd truly be no better than everyone expected her to be: silent, good-natured Regina, who went along to get along, who never thought things through, just acted on impulse like an irresponsible child who needed monitoring.

She placed her glass solidly down on the table and gripped it. Toni and Victoria jumped.

"You know something, not once did either of you ask me why. Not once did either of you ask what you could do. The first thing that came to your minds was, Regina's gone off the deep end again. Doesn't know what she's doing. Well, you know what? I may be the only one who does."

She turned on Toni. "You, great savior of the down-trodden, you're so busy doling out advice you need to take a look in your own backyard. It's always easy to take over someone else's life when you've lost control of your own. And, Ms. Vicky, high and mighty, your idea of success has nothing to do with being happy on the inside, only what people can see on the outside. All appearances, all superficial. There's nothing there, Vicky. Nothing beneath the surface. You two claim to be my friends. When was the last time you were my friends when I needed someone?"

She breathed hard to keep from shaking. "Since we're being so honest, since I need to be put in check, for once I'm doing what I need to do for me." She jabbed at her chest. "But I don't think either of you will ever have what it takes to do the same. You'd rather live in your make-believe worlds where everything is beautiful. But guess what, it isn't. Not until you both see it for what it is."

She pushed back from the table and stood. "I'm not the one to feel sorry for. I feel sorry for the both of you!"

She'd snatched up her purse from the table and walked off, leaving them both with their mouths agape.

A couple entering the restaurant bumped into her, jarring her from her turn of thoughts. Wow, she mused. She'd really let them have it. She gave a little shudder when she thought of that night and the things she'd said to them. It seemed like light-years ago, so much had happened since then, but it had only been a matter of months. Life . . . funny.

And now here she stood ready to do verbal battle once again if need be, but this time she wasn't going to hesitate with what she had to say. They all had their dirty laundry, they'd just have to throw it all in the same machine together and hope that they were able to wash away much of the grime.

Regina rose up on tiptoe to peek over bobbing heads to see if she could spot Toni or Victoria. She knew wherever Vikki was she'd be sitting. She was ready to pop any day now. She caught sight of Toni, who stood up and waved from a table in the back. Regina wound her way in and out of bodies until she reached the table.

"Whew, that was like running the gauntlet," she said, a bright smile on her face. She came around the table and gave Toni a big hug. "How you doing, girl?"

"I'll tell you both all about it."

"Can't wait."

"And you, miss." She turned to Victoria, who was absolutely radiant. "You know, you need to stand up so I can see that tummy."

"Girl, as long as it took me to get my big behind seated, the next time I get up it will be to wobble to the bathroom . . . as usual."

They all broke out in laughter and it was just like old times.

The trio shared a giant bowl of Cesar salad while they waited for their main courses, and Victoria wanted sweet pickles on hers, to which Regina and Toni made identical "yick" faces.

"So you have to tell us what stunt you pulled to get Charles back in the house," Victoria said, plopping a pickle in her mouth. "And don't tell me he fell for the old suicide-by-sleeping-pill trick."

"If you weren't so fat . . ." Toni said.

Regina chuckled. "Vic, you need to stop. This is

serious stuff. Go 'head, Toni, tell us what happened."

"Well, first and foremost, it is totally and forever over between me and Alan. That was a major mistake from the beginning, but my head was in the wrong place at the time and I acted like a fool. Jeopardized everything and nearly lost my husband."

"You still haven't told us how you got that man to take your crazy behind back," Victoria teased.

Toni huffed. "By being honest with myself and with Charles," she said simply and looked from Regina to Victoria. "No matter what the cost of that honesty was."

"So how is everything else?" Regina asked. "The job . . . counseling?"

"I've been seeing a counselor on my own and Charles and I have been going together. It really has helped. I've been cleared to go back to work, but I'm thinking about taking another month. I'm not sure yet. I'm taking everything in stride." She raised her glass in toastlike fashion and took a sip of her wine. "And what about you, Ms. Pregnant Almighty?"

"Neither one of you told me being pregnant was going to be like this."

"Be like what?" Regina asked.

"Amazing." She grinned like a kid. "It is truly amazing."

"Well, we would have but you weren't trying to hear anything about birthin' no babies, remember?" Toni said.

"Yeah, yeah, I remember." She looked at her

friends. "I remember a lot of things, like being a real bitch to you, Regina, and dismissing you out of hand, Toni, but meanwhile I had my own demons to beat."

"Hey, but you did, sis," Regina said. "That's the important thing."

"Finding my real family has been such an awakening, a blessing. I feel as if a part of my soul is complete now. I know most if not all of my issues came from me hating myself. Not ever feeling that I was worthy to have anything of value in my life, not even you two—not that you're all that valuable, but . . ."

Both Toni and Regina hurled their linen napkins at Victoria simultaneously.

"Hey! Hold up. There has to be some kind of law about attacking a pregnant woman in a fancy restaurant," she wailed in feigned distress, waving her white napkin in surrender.

"Is everything all right, ladies?" a concerned-looking waiter asked.

They all looked up at him with innocent wide-eyed expressions. "Everything is fine," they sing-songed off-key.

The trio could barely contain their giggles when he walked away.

"See?" Victoria complained. "You two are going to get us kicked out."

"Oh, you mean like you almost kicked Phillip's secretary out to the curb?" Toni said and started laughing.

"Please don't get me started and make me have this baby in the restaurant. That woman was totally out of her mind," Victoria said.

"I heard you had to go *hood* on her," Regina joined in.

Victoria leaned forward and lowered her voice. "I didn't think I had it in me, but when I found out I had a ball."

"We all have a little bit of the hood in us, just depends on when we need to break it out," Toni said, then turned to Regina. "So what has been going on with you, girl?"

Regina pushed out a long breath. "Wow, where do I begin? I guess I should get this out of the way first so that I can move on. I almost slept with Russell, but common sense jumped in and rescued me."

Toni's and Victoria's mouths and eyes opened fully.

"Get outta here," Toni said. "And you were talking about *me* being all hot and bothered." She tsked.

"Like I said, nothing happened. And I finally put all the brakes on Russell once and for all. He understands that I'm in love with Parker . . . a realization that I didn't fully come to until he told me to get tested for HIV." She looked from one frozen expression to the other, then slowly rolled out the details of what had been going on for the past few months, including Kelly, the kids, and Parker's proposal.

"Damn, girl, no wonder you always save your stories till last!" Toni said.

Victoria tossed her head back and laughed. "Even you can't top that one, T." She slapped Toni's arm and then suddenly grabbed it.

"What's wrong?" Regina asked, seeing the startled expression on Victoria's face.

"My water just broke."

"Hot damn," Toni said, slapping the table. "We're going to be aunties!"

Chapter 37

The average spectator would have thought that a child of royalty was being born. The waiting room was packed with all of Victoria's friends and family. Toni and Regina totally fell in love with Victoria's niece and her mother and father's southern charm.

Steven and Darren and Michele and Tracy, who'd become fast friends, were all busy snacking on chips and reciting bad song lyrics while discussing the latest scandal in the music industry.

Charles and Parker were taking bets on whether it would be a boy or a girl and whether Phillip would pass out in the delivery room or not.

About two hours into the wait, a limp but glowing Phillip emerged covered in a hospital gown. He grinned like the proud papa.

"We have a girl!"

Everyone hugged, shouted, and jumped up and down.

"You owe me five bucks, man," Parker said to Charles, thumping him on the back.

"They're bringing her out now. You can see her through the nursery window," Phillip said. He led the cavalcade to the nursery.

As everyone stood around marveling at the child that Victoria and Phillip brought into the world, Regina relaxed against the hard lines of Parker's side as he held her protectively against him, periodically dropping light kisses on her forehead. While she watched the scene unfold before her, she realized something quite significant.

This day, this new birth was symbolic of new beginnings, journeys yet unseen, filled with hope as well as obstacles. Each person standing there had begun a new journey. No one knew what their future would hold. All any of them could do was open their hearts and minds to possibility and promise and say yes to living life to its fullest.

Regina turned to look up at Parker. "Remember when you asked me to tell you when I was ready?" she asked.

He nodded, hoping that it would be the words he'd longed to hear.

"I have your answer."

"Tell me. Say the words to me, Gina."

"Yes, Parker Heywood." She leaned up and kissed him, long and slow, not caring about the tiny giggles she knew were coming from the kids. She loved him, deep down in her gut she loved him. And whatever lay ahead for them they would deal with it together, for now and always.

She eased back and saw that same love reflected in his eyes. She took his face in her hands. "I say yes," she whispered.

Donna Hill introduces readers to Regina Everett, a gutsy unforgettable heroine they will applaud from the first page to the last—a woman who boldly, blindly, dares to trade a lifestyle for a life . . .

If I Could

In stores now

Turn the page for an excerpt from *If I Could* . . .

CHAPTER ONE

*P*regnant! She should be happy, damn it. It was a miracle. And she was happy—almost—off and on. What sucked the joy out of it was that she knew what this was going to cost her and she had no one to blame but herself. At least she was married, she reasoned. She wouldn't be a statistic. *But, damn, why now?* She grabbed her knapsack, slung it over her shoulder, and jogged down the stairs and out into the bitter November afternoon.

A light snow had begun to fall as Regina got behind the wheel of her brand-new 1985 Toyota Celica and pulled away from the Columbia University campus on Broadway and 120th Street. Her heart beat just a bit faster. Bad weather meant bad traffic and a long trip home. Russell was always more disagreeable if he arrived home before she did. She glanced heavenward. *Please don't let this weather get worse.*

By the time she'd reached the Triborough Bridge, a bare ten minutes later, a steady stream of pure white enveloped all in its path and traffic slowed to a crawl. It would be beautiful to look at, and maybe even enjoy—

some other time. But today she was tired, bone tired, mentally and physically, and her day was nowhere near ending. The nerve beneath her right eye began to tic. She still had to pick up her daughter from her mother's house and get home to prepare dinner for Russell, a task he refused to do even if he was home all day—along with laundry, cleaning, and food shopping. All no-no's in Russell Everette's book. Not to mention taking care of their two-year-old daughter, Michele.

"That's your job, Gina. You wanted to go back to school, to fulfill whatever it is you think you need to fulfill, so you figure out how you're going to get everything done that needs to be taken care of around here," he'd told her in no uncertain terms when she'd asked for some help around the house. "That's the problem with women these days: they want all this independence and equal rights and then when they get them, everything else suffers."

"Russell, I just want to do something for myself besides sit home all day and watch television and think about what to cook for dinner," she said, looking at her hands instead of into his eyes, wishing that for once he would hear her, really hear her.

"Don't I take care of you and Michele, Gina? Aren't I a good husband and father? I bought you a beautiful house, give you enough money so you *don't* have to be out in that rat race, and it's not enough. I don't understand it, Gina. You have the luxury of staying home to raise our child, something that children nowadays desperately need. You and I talked about this," he quickly reminded her. "And you still complain. Do you know how many women would love to be in your shoes?"

The weight of an unnamed guilt settled and lodged in her throat. She twisted her hands in her lap and swallowed over it. "I know . . . it's just that . . ." She glanced up at him and recognized the censorious expression on his face.

"Just what?"

"Nothing. You're right." She shook her head in dismissal. "I can handle it."

"You're going to have to. I *let* you make this decision to go back to school, so you deal with it."

Regina sighed as she reached over the visor and took out her money for the toll. Absently she thanked the clerk for her change and gingerly pulled off, momentarily wishing that there was someplace else for her to go besides home. But that was ridiculous, of course. She was a wife and mother. And wives and mothers didn't have thoughts of leaving their husbands and children. Especially pregnant wives and mothers.

Pregnant. For an instant she relished in the momentary wonder of it. But just as quickly, that euphoric sensation of knowing she carried the life of another within her disappeared in a single breath. She'd have to tell Russell sooner rather than later, and she knew he would put an instant stop to her pursuit of finding herself.

She'd been back in school for six months, and it felt like ten years. At twenty-three, she wasn't the oldest student in her journalism classes but she felt like she was. More days than she cared to count, she wanted to just chuck the whole thing and return home to curl up in front of the soaps and the court TV shows and think about some exotic meal to cook instead. Maybe Russell was right. He always was, and her mother, too. This whole school thing *was* a stupid idea. What was she trying to prove anyway? All it was doing was draining her energy and straining her relationship with her husband.

She was lucky to have a man like Russell, a man

who made sure that his home and family were taken care of. Even her two best friends, Antoinette and Victoria, said so. Then why was she so unhappy?

When she'd married Russell three years earlier she was completely fascinated by him—his looks, his take-charge personality, and a sexiness that rolled off of him in waves. He was striking in appearance: tall, built like a seasoned athlete, and with the smooth, dark brown complexion that she'd always longed for. Everywhere he went women took second looks, but he had eyes only for her—a phenomenon that fascinated her almost more than he did. She knew she wasn't bad-looking. Not really. But she was certainly no raving beauty. She struggled with her fluctuating weight all her life—and having a baby only added to the problem. She still maintained fifteen pounds she couldn't seem to shake. She had pimple breakouts whenever she became too stressed—which seemed to be too often lately—and she tended to be quiet and reserved—a trait that was just part of who she was, but unnerved the people around her. Yet right from the beginning, Russell didn't seem to care about any of those things. He would take her shopping and pick out clothes he said would suit her figure, and send her to the hair salon whenever he thought her hair wasn't just right. He bought her all kinds of creams and lotions for her skin and even set up an appointment with a skin specialist, who he assured her would help with her problem.

Regina was touched by his kindness, his thoughtfulness, and the attention he paid to her. She was accustomed to having someone manage her life for her, make her decisions—know what was best for her. That was all she'd known, from her overbearing, overprotective mother, to Catholic school, where the nuns ruled with an iron fist and reminded you daily about hell and

damnation, and any unique thought or action was considered sacrilegious. Russell's entrance into her life
was only more of the same. He took care of her, took
the pressure of daily living off her shoulders and onto
his. But he came with the added benefit of being a
man, a man who awakened the sleeping giant of her
sexuality—who made her feel like a woman. It was the
only area of her life where she felt she mattered—in
which she participated and was appreciated.

She shivered, uncertain if it was from the cold, or
from the fleeting erotic thoughts of her husband's touch,
their nights together, the heights they reached, and her
growing feelings of worthlessness and shame the
mornings after.

Often she wished that she could share her traitorous
feelings with Vicky and Toni, but she couldn't. They
had perfect lives, great careers, came off as being sure
of themselves, and knew what they wanted from life.
She couldn't stand to be diminished in their eyes. She
wanted to belong. She wanted what they had, or at least
wanted to pretend that she did. How could she ever
admit that things were not as they seemed? Not to
them. And the more alone she felt in her marriage, the
tighter she clung to their friendship.

Regina turned on the radio in the hopes of tuning
out her troubling thoughts, but that served only to
muddy them for the moment. If she could just hang on
for three more months, she thought, she would have
her master's degree, and the editor at the *Daily News,*
where she was doing her internship, assured her he'd
take her on full-time. He liked her work, thought she
had a lot of potential and a keen eye for detail. "I think
you'll make one helluva reporter one day, Regina," he'd
said. But how long would that last once her pregnancy
became obvious? *Damn!*

Finally, after a grueling two-hour, stop-and-go, slip-and-slide trip that should have been no more than forty-five minutes, she eased into her mother's driveway in St. Albans.

Reluctantly she shut off the engine of her Toyota, stepped out of the car, and her bootless feet sank into a layer of icy white snow. She inched her way to her mom's front door, instinctively wary of falling and the harm it could present to the budding life she carried. Maybe a new baby would soften Russell a bit, change his attitude about his role and hers in the house, she mused. He had to give her some assistance with a toddler in the house and another baby on the way. She couldn't imagine that his macho attitude would overrule her and the baby's health. He'd been an absolute Prince Charming when she was pregnant with Michele. There wasn't enough he could do for her.

She silently prayed for those days of bliss-filled happiness to return to the Everette household. In the meantime, she must deal with her mother and the lecture she was sure she'd receive about something the instant she set foot across the threshold. She stuck her key in the door and switched her mind to "off."

As always her mother's neat little house was in immaculate condition. Every item was in its place, every surface was clear and dust free, and the air smelled as fresh as springtime. And as always, even moving toward the dinner hour, Millicent Prescott looked as if she'd just stepped off the cover of a magazine. Her red-brown skin was perfectly made up, not a hair was out of place, and her still-trim body was stylish in a designer pantsuit in a soft mocha that did wonderful things for her light brown eyes—the only trait Regina had acquired from her mother. She felt an overwhelming need to check her own reflection in the mirror. Her mother had a way of doing that to her—making her feel self-conscious and vulnerable without uttering one word. It was in the unflinching set of her eyes and her strident attitude.

"Hi, Mom. Sorry I'm late." She dropped the keys in her purse and walked toward her mother, her arms outstretched for Michele.

Millicent's mouth was drawn into a tight line.

Michele started to tear away from her grandmother's hand and dart toward her mother, when Millicent's no-nonsense voice halted her in her toddler tracks. "What did Grandma say about running?" Her voice cracked like a whip. The little girl turned wide eyes on her grandmother. "Little girls don't run; they walk—like ladies. Remember?" she said a bit more softly, making direct eye contact with Michele, then gave her a tender kiss on her cheek. "That's my girl," she said in her sweetest voice, the voice that always came after the tongue-lashing that soothed the sting, the one you longed to hear to make your wrong go away.

She stared at Regina while talking to her granddaughter. "I'm sure your mommy doesn't allow you to run." Her smile missed her eyes. "I taught her better than that."

Regina's insides suddenly heaved as waves of unforgotten childhood anxiety swept through her. She breathed deeply, pushing them away as Michele walked ladylike into her arms. "Hi, sweetie," she whispered into her cottony soft hair. She held her tight against her chest for a moment. *Michele, the one thing she'd done right in her life.*

Millicent crossed the room, her posture impeccable. "That poor child just goes from hand to hand," she moaned in that martyred way of hers that curled the hairs on the back of Regina's neck. "You know how much I love that baby—and you—but there's no reason on God's green earth why this baby should be traipsing across town all kinds of hours when she could just as well be home with her mother."

"Mom, please. We've been through this a million times. I'm in school. I need a sitter so that I can go. You said you would do it, that you didn't mind," she went on, going down the list. "I don't want to leave Michele with just anyone and you know that."

"I really don't see why you can't wait until this child is older before you do whatever it is that you're doing. It's ridiculous and so selfish of you, Regina." She pressed her hand to her chest. "I would cry every day when I had to go out to work and leave you. I only wish I'd had the kind of husband who could have taken care of the two of us. If he could, I wouldn't have been forced to work, to leave my only child every day to be raised by strangers." Her entire expression tightened, making her smooth, brown face and sharp Indian features appear as if they'd suddenly been cast in plaster. She turned mournful eyes on her only child. "You have everything I ever dreamed of, Regina. I made sure of that." She stepped closer. "A husband who loves you, provides handsomely for you, takes care of everything so that you don't have a worry in the world, a beautiful daughter. You owe him a lot. Sweetheart, don't ruin that. Family comes first. You have time to pursue these dreams of yours. Think of your daughter, your husband." She lowered her voice, as if afraid that some unseen person would overhear. "Russell talks to me, Regina. He always has. You know he's like a son to me." She paused. "He's not happy, Regina, not happy at all. I can't blame him. And unhappy men . . ." Millicent arched a finely tapered brow.

Regina's stomach tightened. She knew very well

what her mother was implying. She lifted Michele into her arms and pushed out a long, exasperated breath. "Well, this may all be a moot point, anyway," Regina said, feeling the cape of defeat settle around her shoulders.

"What are you saying?"

Regina shook her head. At least for now her secret was one thing she could call her own. She could savor this one bit of happiness awhile longer. "I'll talk to Russell," she said on a breath. "We'll work it out."

"I certainly hope so," Millicent said with a note of skepticism in her voice. She loved her daughter—there was no question about that; she'd sacrificed more than she could ever hope to regain to ensure that Regina had everything. During those years when her own marriage began to crumble, all she had was Regina, her daughter, her baby girl. They built their worlds around each other, just the two of them, and she prepared Regina as best she could to be ready for the life of a good wife and mother. Russell was the perfect man for Regina; she knew it the instant she met him through a former coworker. He was strong, driven, knew what he wanted and how to get it. So much like her own husband, Robert, had once been. Russell was just the kind of man her daughter needed, someone who could continue to guide and care for her with a strong hand, the way she had done. She knew her daughter possessed nothing exceptional in looks; men didn't flock around her, so her choices weren't bountiful. There was no way that she would let Russell get away.

But they were both worried about her now. Neither of them understood this phase she was going through. Millicent was certain it would pass. If there was one thing she knew about her daughter, it was that she wouldn't resist what she knew was right. And being there for her family was the right thing. Women sacrificed, that's what they did, and the sooner Regina accepted that, the happier she would be.

Regina focused her attention on getting Michele into her snowsuit and out of her mother's house. She was suffocating, the air of her own thoughts sucked out of her. It was hard to explain how she felt each time she stepped across the threshold of the home of her youth, other than to say that she felt like a child, incapable and inexperienced, and she behaved accordingly. And as much as she understood that this bizarre transformation did take place, she was no more able to do anything about it than she could fly without a plane. That knowledge ate away at her day by day.

Hauling a bundled Michele up into her arms, she headed for the door. "I'll call you during the weekend, Mom."

"I was hoping you and Russell would come by for Sunday dinner. I'll fix your favorite, macaroni and cheese casserole," she cajoled. "You know how lonely I get over the weekend. There's nothing worse than eating alone." Then she suddenly waved her hand in dismissal. "No, no. You have dinner with your own family. I'll be just fine. Whatever I fix will just have to serve me for the week. Don't you worry. I'll be fine," she repeated. Her eyes seemed to have lost their sparkle, and the forlorn, downward curve of her mouth was not lost on Regina.

Regina sighed. "Sure, we'll come. I'm sure Russell would love it anyway."

Millicent perked right up, just as Regina had known she would. Millicent clapped her hands together. "Wonderful. I'll fix all your favorite foods and that pound cake Russell loves so much. And I'll get to see my baby again." She cooed and gurgled, nuzzling Michele's cheek.

"I gotta go, Mom. I'll call you."

"Drive safely, sweetheart. You know how you are when you get yourself upset."

Regina tugged in a breath. "I'm not upset, Mother."

Millicent, ignoring her comment, pecked Regina's cheek, then held it in the palm of her hand. "You know I love you, Regina. I only want the best for you," she said in that patronizing tone that made Regina want to shake her. "Don't damage this marriage of yours. Talk to Russell; try to see his side in all this." Her gaze ran a quick inventory over her daughter. "I see your face is breaking out again, and you could use a touch-up," she added, rubbing the roots of Regina's hair between her fingers.

By now she could hardly breathe at all; it was like those horrid times when her mother would make her play piano in front of all of her card-playing friends on Saturday nights when she'd just learned the piece the day before. She'd feel all clammy, her head would pound, and her heart would race as if it would burst from her chest. But she played anyway, because she slowly began to realize that the sooner she did what her mother demanded, the sooner she could breathe again.

She stepped outside and gulped in a lungful of air.

Regina carried her overdressed, sleeping two-year-old daughter on her hip, draped Michele's baby bag over one shoulder and her duffel bag of books on the other. She entered the house from the side door that opened onto the kitchen. And of course it was empty. Not even the sound of boiling water could be detected in the spotless kitchen. She shouldn't have expected anything different—but, damn it, maybe just once.

Huffing with her load, she let her bag fall with a dull thud onto the jade green marble floor. Russell would just have to fuss, she thought, her frustration and weariness beginning to take a toll on her. Michele whimpered and shifted her body, nearly causing Regina to lose her grip. She hoisted the sleeping baby a bit higher on her hip and mounted the stairs to the bedrooms above.

She heard water coming from the shower in the master bath as she gingerly tried to undress Michele without waking her.

"Just getting in?" Russell's heavy baritone crept up behind her.

She stiffened, keeping her back to him, and finished undressing her daughter. "Yes," she mumbled. "Traffic is pretty bad with the snow." She put a light blanket over Michele and tiptoed away. When she turned, Russell's imposing frame blocked the doorway. He looked down at her.

"Why are you doing this, Regina?"

She blew out a breath and stood her ground. "Doing what?" Really, she didn't want to have this conversation again—not today. She'd exhausted all the reasons to justify her "rebellious" behavior, as her friend Antoinette called it. Vicky just called it plain stupid. "Why go through all that drama if you don't have to? If the man wants to take care of you, let him."

"You know what I'm talking about, Regina," he said, cutting into her train of thought. "This whole school thing, not being home, so involved with books and papers that you don't have time for me—and for Godsake the newspaper." He turned away in disgust and headed for the bedroom. Regina followed and shut the door behind her.

"I'm doing the best I can, Russ."

He spun to face her. "The best you can," he said incredulously. "You're kidding me, right? You can spread yourself just so thin before something finally snaps, Regina."

"Maybe things wouldn't snap if you didn't place the whole responsibility of this family, this house, this marriage on me. You're a part of this, too. Doesn't it matter to you what I want, what I need?"

"As long as I'm the provider, as long as I take care of you and my child, then yes, the rest is up to you. And as for what you need and want, I don't think you know what that is. You said you wanted to be married, raise a family. But you don't act like it. You're acting like our marriage and this family are the last things on your list. An afterthought."

"That's not true."

"Isn't it? Tell me why it's not. I want to hear this for myself." He folded his arms and waited.

Suddenly she had a flash of the nuns from grammar school, waiting for her to explain why she'd missed Sunday mass. It didn't matter what explanation you gave—short of death—you were wrong and you would be punished accordingly. That's how she felt now, that no matter what she said it wouldn't make a difference. But she had to try, just as she had all those years ago. And she would take her punishment in stoic silence, and think up another reason to give the next time. There was always a next time. She would make sure of it by playing sick on Sunday morning, oversleeping or taking too long to get dressed. It was the one time when she could feel in control, feel significant—just for those few moments.

"I want to be a whole person, with outside interests," she finally said. "I want to be able to talk to people about more than recipes, household tips, and diaper rash. I'm good at what I do, Russell, but you never notice. You don't want to notice. Not once have you ever asked me how my classes are, what I do at the *News*. Never."

"I know you're good at what you do. I don't need to ask you. Why do you think I miss your touch around here?"

"Russell—"

"Shhh." He stepped up to her. "Hey, careers, this school thing, there's plenty of time for that. We need to concentrate on us. You got time."

"Russell, it's not going to get easier." She moved away from him and sat on the bed.

"Ask any of your friends what they would do if they had a choice." He sat beside her. She eased away. He put his arm around her and she shuddered. Russell smiled in anticipation.

"Russell, this isn't about my friends. It's—"

His mouth covered hers, silencing her. Her body stiffened. He pulled her closer. "Baby, I want us to work," he breathed deep in her ear, his hot breath flooding her in waves. "But I need your help."

"Russell, just listen to me."

"We have all the time in the world to talk." His fingers began playing with the back of her neck, and electric waves ran along her spine. She sucked in air through her nose and held it in her chest. He pushed her baby soft hair aside and kissed her behind her ear, then in it. Her eyes slid close, and she silently screamed.

"I'd do anything for you," he said in a hoarse whisper. "You know that, don't you?"

"Yes." And she felt sick inside as her body began to involuntarily heat against her will.

"Then let me, baby. Let me take care of you." He ran his hand across her breast. She pulled back and he took it as a tease. He laughed deep in his throat.

"Russell . . . please . . . !"

"I know—me, too." He covered her mouth again and eased her down on the queen-size bed. He unbuttoned her plain white blouse and unzipped her jeans.

Her body weakened, softened as it always did, betraying her. She knew she was saying the words, but he couldn't hear her. She was telling him to stop, she knew she was, but it was pointless. He wouldn't hear her even if she screamed. It was always this way between them. He'd cut off her thoughts, stop her words, by filling her body with his. And she was helpless to resist. She hated this part of herself more than anything, this weak, needy part that begged to be heard. This part of her that sang in the pleasure of his touch, for his connection to her, even as her mind tried to resist, even as the unspeakable rush of her climax held her, shook her until tears of anguish streamed from her eyes.

"Yeah," he said with a groan, "that's my baby. You're mine. No one can make you feel like this," he ground out through his teeth.

He was right, she thought through the haze as yet another apex ripped through her. She needed this, needed to feel this—this one thing in her life that made her believe she was capable of anything—if only for a moment. If she closed her eyes, let the sensations flow through her, she became powerful, strong, visible. She was beautiful and desirable. With a thrust of her hips she could weaken him. She could be heard if she cried out his name, moaned in pleasure. He understood all that. If only for a moment.

Russell shuddered once, twice, before his body collapsed atop her. He didn't say a word, didn't share a tender touch, a thought. He simply rolled over and quickly fell into a satiated sleep.

Regina curled into a ball, pressing her fist to her

mouth to keep from howling like a wounded animal. She turned her head, looked over her shoulder at her sleeping husband. She should feel something—anything. Her body still tingled, satisfied beyond words, but her heart and soul were so very empty, needy.

Tears of sadness rolled down her cheeks as she thought of the child she carried, the sleeping baby in the next room, the vows spoken before God and man, and she wondered how she would get through the rest of her life if everything in it didn't change.

More of the Hottest
African-American Fiction from
Dafina Books

Come With Me J.S. Hawley	0-7582-1935-0	$6.99/$9.99
Golden Night Candice Poarch	0-7582-1977-6	$6.99/$9.99
No More Lies Rachel Skerritt	0-7582-1601-7	$6.99/$9.99
Perfect For You Sylvia Lett	0-7582-1979-2	$6.99/$9.99
Risk Ann Christopher	0-7582-1434-0	$6.99/$9.99

Available Wherever Books Are Sold!

Visit our website at **www.kensingtonbooks.com**.